I0788789

# TRIGGER PULL

# TRIGGER PULL

---

## THE SILENCER SERIES BOOK 10

## MIKE RYAN

WWW.MIKERYANBOOKS.COM

**1**

———

Recker had another restless sleep. Ever since he'd gotten back from London, he could count on one hand the amount of times he actually felt refreshed and re-energized after waking up. It seemed every night was a new nightmare. Almost all of them involved something bad happening. Whether it was to him, Mia, Jones, or Haley, it seemed one of them was always passing away in the dream. And it was usually violently.

Most of the time, he didn't remember much about the dream. Just the end result. Though the others were occasionally in them, by far the nightmare he had the most, involved himself. Sometimes it was him falling off a tall building, sometimes he'd turn around and get shot by some unknown assailant, usually not even seeing their face, and sometimes it was him lying in some cold, dark alley, the rain pelting the back of his dead body.

Recker sat on the edge of the bed, his elbows on his

knees as he put his hands on top of his head. He was tired and trying to shake the images of his dead corpse out of his mind. He looked back at Mia's spot in the bed, but all that was left was her sunken pillow and rumpled blanket. He put his nose in the air and could smell her making breakfast. He grabbed his phone off the nightstand and stumbled out to the kitchen.

Before doing anything else, Recker came up behind Mia and put his arms around her waist, hugging her and kissing her on the neck. She turned around and kissed his lips. They spent another couple of minutes embracing, neither feeling the need to say a word. After they were done, Mia playfully pushed his chest so they could begin eating.

"Sit down and eat your breakfast," she told him, bringing his plate over.

Still without knowing what time it was, Recker sat down and checked his phone. It was earlier than he thought it was, being only a few minutes after seven. By the sun shining in through the window he assumed it to be around nine o'clock or so. Though the sunshine was supposed to help increase people's moods and make them feel better, it sure didn't seem to do much for him. He felt as grumpy as if he hadn't gone to bed at all. The only thing that was keeping him from showing it was the beautiful woman sitting across from him. He certainly didn't want to bring her down with him.

It was a quiet morning by their standards. They spent the next few minutes eating, not even saying a word to each other. They usually were pretty talkative with what they had planned for the day, so this morning was quite unusual for them. Recker kept his head down as he was eating, staring at his food. Mia kept looking at him, wondering when or if he was going to say something. She already thought she knew but wanted him to say it. She'd often wake up multiple times during the night, hearing Recker mumble in his sleep, or feel him toss and turn constantly. Though she rarely said anything about it, she could tell he was having bad dreams a lot. After a few more minutes, she finally had enough of the silence and knew she'd have to drag it out of him, just like usual.

"You gonna say anything today?"

Recker stopped playing with his food and looked up. "Huh?"

"You haven't said a word all morning."

"Oh. Sorry. Guess I just have things on my mind."

"Anything you wanna talk about?"

Recker shook his head as he went back to playing with his food. "No, not really."

Mia let out a very loud sigh, intending for Recker to hear her displeasure.

"You OK?" Recker asked, more concerned with her well-being than his own.

"No, not really."

"What's the matter? You feel alright?"

"You're what's the matter."

"What'd I do?"

"You won't talk to me," Mia replied.

"What do you wanna talk about?"

"How about we start with what's bothering you?"

"There's nothing bothering me."

Mia gave him a displeased look as she tilted her head, clearly not happy with his answer. Recker raised his eyebrows before looking back down at his food, not wanting to look at her. He didn't like seeing her mad at him, which she now clearly seemed to be at the moment.

"Mike, you've been having bad dreams for nearly a month now."

"I'm fine."

"Really? Then why do you wake up in the middle of the night sometimes sweating? Or you sit on the edge of the bed with your hands on your head. You toss and turn more times than I can count. And sometimes you talk incoherently."

Recker looked almost embarrassed that she knew all that. "I didn't realize you were watching my every move."

"It's hard not to when you appear to be in as much discomfort as you are."

"I'm OK," Recker said, not wanting to make a big deal of it.

Mia got up and moved to the chair next to him, hoping to convince him to come clean with her. She put her hand on the back of his head and rubbed it. "Why don't you just tell me what it is? Maybe I can help you get through it?"

Recker turned his head to look at her. He smiled, wondering how he was lucky enough to end up with someone like her. She was definitely the best part of his life. He stumbled over his words at first, not knowing how to begin.

"I don't know what it is. Every night it's a new night-mare. Or it's an old nightmare."

"What about?" Mia asked.

Recker rubbed the side of his head as he cleared his throat, not wanting to get too specific. "Usually the same thing. Somebody dying."

"Anyone specific?"

"Always someone I know. David, Chris... a few times it was you," he said, looking at her and trying to plaster a smile on his face to disguise how concerned he was. Not that it worked though. "But mostly it's been me."

Mia continued rubbing the back of his head and also leaned in to kiss his cheek. "They're only dreams."

"I know, but..."

Mia continued to try to ease his fears. "They're not going to come true if that's what's bothering you. They're just dreams. Nothing more."

"What if it's a sign of something?"

"Like what?"

Recker shrugged. "Maybe it's a sign that I'm... broken. Like maybe everything's finally catching up to me. Maybe it's a signal that something's gonna happen soon."

Mia put both of her hands on the sides of Recker's face as she looked deep into his eyes. There was a look in them that she hadn't seen before. Maybe it was fear. Maybe it was sadness. She couldn't quite put her finger on it. They just looked different somehow. They put their foreheads together as they closed their eyes, just letting the moment settle in. Then Mia brought her head inches from Recker's, their noses almost touching as she tried to console him.

"Nothing is going to happen to you. Everything is not predetermined. The dreams are not indicating that you're going to die soon. You're in control of everything. No one else."

Recker tried to give her a warm smile, though it came off as a half-hearted attempt. Mia kissed him, then the two engaged in a long embrace. Recker wasn't yet sure if the talk worked. He still felt a little different. He couldn't pinpoint what it was either, but something inside him just didn't feel right. Maybe it was something that would pass once he got to work and put all this stuff behind him. At least until the next day, when he was sure he'd wake up from a similar dream.

After releasing each other, they stared into each other's eyes for a few moments. Recker put his hands on her arms and rubbed them up and down. She was such an amazing person, he thought. Sometimes he still wasn't sure what he did to deserve her. But here they were, her doing everything in her power to make him feel better and lift her spirits. Suddenly, as he stared at her, his thoughts turned from his own dreams to thoughts of her.

"What about you?" Recker asked. "Are you OK?"

"I'm fine, why?"

Recker briefly glimpsed down at her stomach. "You know, the baby."

Mia's eyes quickly became glossy as she fought to hold back the tears. They hadn't talked about it in about two weeks. For the first few days after Recker got home from

Europe, though Mia was happy to have him back, she still felt an unbelievable sense of sadness. Even when he was there, she found herself sitting alone in their room sometimes. Though they talked about it, and Recker tried to be understanding and do what he could for her, it was something she had to work out on her own. He would never be able to understand what that must have felt like. All he could do was try to be there for her when she needed him, which he was.

After about a week, her sadness and depression started to fade, and she thrust herself back into her work, getting a few more double shifts than usual. Though she usually fought through the bad thoughts that ran through her mind when Recker was home, it was worse when he wasn't there at all. At least being at work helped to take her mind off it, especially during the day when Recker was usually out doing his thing.

As Mia thought about his question, she didn't feel the need to try to hide her true feelings from him. There wasn't any point in trying to mask them or make herself out to be stronger than she really was. Even so, she still struggled to get the words out. She tried to form a smile, though she wasn't quite able to get one out.

"Some days are better than others," she said. "I don't know if the feelings will ever truly go away. I just feel like something inside is missing. Something should be there, and it isn't. Some days are not too bad, and others, I just wanna bury my head in the sand."

"What can I do?" Recker asked, wishing he could take her pain away.

Mia finally was able to form that smile she'd been trying to put on. She put her arms around Recker's neck and kissed him. "You've already done everything you can. You've been there for me, we've talked, there's nothing else you can do."

"I feel like I can do more. Like I should be doing more."

"There's not. Honestly, just you being here, talking, that's enough. I'm getting better. Day by day, little by little, I'm getting there."

Recker cleared his throat, though it was pretty obvious that he had forced a cough that wasn't really necessary.

"What is it?" Mia asked, recognizing his clues for when he had something to talk about that was uncomfortable for him.

"Umm, well, it's not something we've talked about, and I don't know if you want to right now."

"Now's as good a time as any. As long as it won't make me unhappy. I don't know if I could stand more unhappiness."

"Well, I dunno..."

Mia let out a laugh, thinking it cute how he always danced around awkward subjects. "Just say it."

"I was just thinking... I know I was a little stunned when you told me the first time..."

"A little stunned?"

Recker grinned, knowing he undersold his reaction. "OK. Maybe a lot. But anyway, I was stunned at first, and it took me some time to get used to it, but if the time comes, and I know it's up to you whenever you're ready... but if the time comes and you wanna try again... I would like to."

Mia couldn't contain or hold back her smile this time as she threw her arms around him again, planting a big kiss on his lips. "I love you."

"I love you too."

They began kissing some more, though their affection was interrupted by the sound of Recker's phone going off. He looked at it and the pleasant look on his face was quickly replaced by a look of disgust.

"What is it?" Mia asked.

"It's David. Something's going down. I'm gonna have to go."

Recker got up and quickly got dressed. Once he was ready, he walked over to the door, getting another kiss from his girlfriend before he left.

"Make sure you take care of yourself," Mia said.

Though she would never outwardly say it, she was slightly alarmed by the dreams he was having. Not that she believed they were an indication they were going to come true, but more because she hoped they didn't make him alter his behavior. Recker got this far by trusting his instincts. If the dreams he was having him bothered him so much that he started to doubt those instincts, that's what worried her more.

"Don't worry, I'll be back," Recker said.

"You better."

**2**

———

Recker had just started driving when he called Jones to see what was going on. There was no point in going to the office and wasting time if Recker could get to wherever he needed to go to quicker from where he already was.

"What's up?" Recker asked.

"We appear to have a kidnapping in progress."

"What's the status?"

"When I say in progress, I literally mean in progress," Jones answered.

"Why are we just hearing about it now?"

"We're not. I've been tracking these guys for the better part of two weeks. The problem was that they weren't communicating with any details up to now. Just generalities. I'm not sure they knew either. But today, the apparent leader of the group let the others know it was happening now."

"How much time we got?"

"You probably have none," Jones said. "Chris, though, might be able to make it in time. I dispatched him about ten minutes ago, so hopefully he'll be able to get there." Jones then gave Recker the address that he wanted him to go to.

"How many people are we dealing with?"

"Three as far as I can determine."

"Histories?"

"All have violence in their backgrounds. They probably won't scare easily so it is likely that you will have to use force."

"What about the target?"

"Fred Pinkston. He's a bank manager for one of the large national brands."

"What are they planning on doing? Using him to open a vault or something?"

"It would appear so. Like I said, they haven't talked specifics that I could determine. So, I would assume instead of going into the bank guns blazing, they're using a more methodical approach. I would say that they probably want to use him for access as well as bypassing security measures."

"Why not just grab him as he gets to the bank or enters the building?" Recker asked.

"Probably because they want to prepare him for what they're planning. Some people feel they're more likely to get cooperation from their victims when they can prepare them in advance for what they want. That way there's less a chance of them panicking at the wrong moment and throwing the entire plan into mayhem."

"Chris gonna be able to get there in time?"

"I'm not sure. Let me check in with him. You hurry up and get there."

"Well, I'm not driving like Miss Daisy."

Jones then called Haley. "Chris, what's your position?"

"Just about there. Couple minutes away."

They continued talking until Haley finally reached his destination three minutes later, a two-story brick home in the northeast part of the city. It was in an affluent area, where most of the residents were swimming in money. Long driveways and plenty of land and distance between neighbors, not usually a plentiful thing in the city, punctuated this area. Haley, driving fast, quickly turned a corner into Pinkston's driveway, a loud screeching noise from the tires sliding on the pavement, and smoke rising into the air. As he drove up to the main house, he saw he was a little bit late. Hopefully not too late. There was already another car in the driveway, and it wasn't the one that Jones said belonged to the owner of the house.

"Another car in sight," Haley said, his car coming to a grinding halt. "Looks like they're already here. Gotta go."

"Do you see them already? What's going on?"

Jones didn't get an answer. Haley had already hung up and was out of the car, running up to the front door. Jones had hoped for at least something of an advanced scouting report, that way he could relay it to Recker, so he knew what he was getting into. But since that was no longer possible, Recker would just have to wing it once he got there. It wouldn't be that much different than usual for him.

Once Haley got to the door, he found that it was slightly ajar and pushed it open. He crouched down, his gun lifted in front of him as he entered the home. Almost immediately after going in he was met with gunfire. A shot ripped off a piece of the door frame as Haley quickly tried to identify his targets. He hid back behind the door for a few seconds to figure out his plan.

From the sound of the gun, he knew they were somewhere in front of him. Haley took another peek around the door and didn't see anyone in sight. He rushed in, once again drawing gunfire. It was coming from the dining room, which was just in front of him. There were two rooms to each side of him, and Haley took cover behind the first thing he saw, which was a small rustic looking chair. It wasn't much of a shield and Haley figured even a plastic bullet probably would've been able to penetrate it.

With a slight break in the firing, Haley stood up and rushed into the dining area. As soon as he entered the room, another man appeared, holding a gun in his hand. As Haley passed him, he was running too fast to realistically stop and face him, so he just kept on going. But as he passed, he swatted the gun out of the man's hand. After successfully knocking the gun out, Haley jumped on top of the dining table and slid to the other side of the rectangular-shaped table, knocking off the centerpiece as he glided along. When he got to the end of it, Haley rolled over and stuck the landing on his knees like he was an Olympic gymnast. In one continuous motion after sliding off the table, Haley quickly identified his first target, the man who had his gun knocked out of his hands, and fired, successfully drilling him with a couple of shots to the chest.

Haley heard another of the men yell out the name of the man he just shot, giving away their location. Haley waited at the end of the table for a moment, sizing things up, waiting to see if the men would come to him first. After a minute or two, Haley figured he'd have to do the stalking. He got up and started moving towards the kitchen area. About halfway there, another man emerged from the room. Haley and the man fired at each other simultaneously, both narrowly missing each other. Haley rebounded first and was able to get the first aim again, shooting the man, but not fatally. The bullet was a through and through in the man's shoulder, not hitting anything of importance and no major damage except for a good amount of blood loss. The man retreated back into the kitchen area as Haley pinned himself to the wall.

Haley took a few deep breaths, then unglued himself from the wall and sped into the kitchen, several bullets being fired at him as he entered, all of which narrowly missed him. Haley ducked behind the counter, waiting a few seconds before raising his head over the countertop. Once he rose up to see where his targets were, exposing his face slightly, he almost got his head shot off, a bullet grazing off the marble granite countertop just an inch away from him.

"Let Pinkston go!" Haley yelled. "You're not getting out of here with him."

"I think we will," a male voice replied. "Still got you outnumbered."

"Only for the moment. We got more guys coming, and you'll be surrounded soon enough. We know about your plan at the bank so you can't even pull that off anymore whether you have Pinkston or not."

Haley could hear the two men remaining talking to each other, though they were speaking so low that he couldn't hear exactly what they were saying.

"By the blood on the floor I know one of you's bleeding pretty bad," Haley said. "Gonna need to get that wound checked out soon unless you wanna lose an arm."

"Just stop talking man!"

"All right, suit yourself."

Haley looked at his watch, wondering if Recker was going to show up soon. He never did find out from Jones whether their partner was on the way or not. Jones told him he was going to call Recker, but it just never came up when Jones called Haley back. It would have been nice to know so he could plan accordingly. Haley felt his pocket for his phone, but he didn't have it on him. He was talking to Jones on the way in and left in a hurry. He must have just tossed it down on the seat of his car when he exited.

"Listen man, we're getting out of here and we're using this dude for a shield, so you better take your finger off the trigger of that gun."

Haley quickly rose up again, putting his elbows on the countertop as he aimed his gun at the intruders. They also had their guns aimed at him as they slowly walked sideways across the kitchen, holding Pinkston in front of them for protection.

"You try anything funny or try to hit one of us and we'll kill him."

"Just let him go now and I give you my word I'll let you leave without a problem," Haley replied.

The leader of the group laughed, not having any of that. "Yeah, right, you think I'm stupid? We let him go and you open up. We're not letting him go until we're safe and sound out of here."

"I'll let you get to your car. You take him with you, and I'll have to follow you."

"You do that and he's as good as dead."

"In that case there's no length I won't go to to bring you down. Your best bet is to just let him go when you hit the front door and then just keep on going."

The men exited the kitchen with their hostage, moving into the living room, Haley following them. He kept as close as possible to them without making himself a wide-open target. He stuck to the walls and then behind furniture once he moved out of the kitchen. The men were still moving slowly with Pinkston, worried about Haley trying to keep them from reaching the door.

As it turned out, they never had to worry about Haley at all. They were so concerned about him, that they never saw the other man waiting at the front door for them. Recker had been standing there for a minute or two, getting there just in time to hear Haley going back and forth with the men in the kitchen. He figured if he stood there long enough, the action would just come to him. No need to even move. He was right.

The men continued backing away from Haley, their backs still to the door. Recker played with them long enough to give them the idea that they just might make it. He disappeared out of sight outside, just beyond the door, standing to the side of it. Gripping his gun firmly in his hand, he waited for the right moment. He'd done this so many times now, there wasn't an ounce or nerves or anxiety. He almost felt too loose, as if nothing could go wrong.

About thirty seconds later, one of the men appeared in the door. He still didn't see Recker since he wasn't all the way through it yet. Thinking he was in the clear since the other guy had the hostage still, the man turned to start running to the car, so he could bring it up to the door and park on the grass to give them an easier exit. He almost got both his feet out the door. Almost.

Recker gunned the man down just before his second foot touched down on the concrete walkway. The leader of the group had also just reached the door, and startled by the shots being fired behind him, let go of his hostage as he jumped, finally turning toward the door. Letting go of Pinkston gave Haley a clear shot, and he took it. The bullet ripped through the upper part of the man's back, closer to his right shoulder. The force of the bullet entering his body made him stumble forward, taking a few steps out the door. Now that he was firmly in Recker's line of sight, The Silencer calmly put one more, fatal slug into his chest. The man fell to the concrete, dead before he even touched it.

Haley went over to check on Pinkston as Recker patiently waited outside. Haley already knew his partner was there without either of them saying a word to confirm it. It would have been no one else. He doubted the police would have been so gun-happy. They would have at least given the men a chance to surrender. Not that they deserved it. As Haley checked on Pinkston, Recker checked his gun and reloaded. He walked back to his car as he waited for his friend to finish up. Haley came walking out a minute later and headed straight for his friend.

"Took you long enough to get here," Haley chided.

Recker smiled. "Well, I knew you had everything well under control. When Jones told me about this, I was actually gonna head to the golf course since I knew you'd take care of this no problem."

Haley couldn't resist a chuckle. "Oh really? Well, I mean, I did do all the heavy lifting here. You got the easy shots at the end."

"That's how you work it when you're the senior member of the team. You let the junior members do the work, then you take the credit for it."

"I'll remember that for whenever I become a senior member."

Putting all kidding aside, Recker finally turned serious. "How's the banker?"

"He's good. A little shaken by everything, but nothing

he won't get over. At least physically anyway. I would imagine after this he'll get an alarm system or something."

"Speaking of alarms, we should probably get moving. Police will probably be here in a minute or two."

"Yeah. Chalk another one up in the books."

**3**

———

Recker and Haley arrived back at the office after their excursion at the Pinkston residence, both plopping down on the couch to relax for a few minutes. Jones peeked up at them over his computer.

"Rough go of it?" Jones asked.

"No, not really," Haley answered. "Wasn't too bad. Nothing out of the ordinary."

"Did you get there in time for the festivities, Michael?"

"Oh yeah. Right at the end. Just in time for the fun to finish up. Got anything else on the agenda?"

"Nothing that requires our immediate attention. I'm just monitoring a few things at the moment. I suspect we're still a day or two away from any of those though."

"Pity."

The room was silent for a few minutes as Recker and Haley sat there relaxing, and Jones did his computer work.

The quiet room was interrupted by the sound of Recker's phone going off.

"What's up, Tyrell?"

"Hey, that was good. You're getting better. It was almost like a hello. One of these days you'll get there."

"You call me for something important or just to rag on my phone conversation skills?"

"Nah, I just wanted to let you know I heard something was brewing. Something big."

"Such as what?"

"Not sure. Don't have many details."

"Well who's involved?" Recker asked.

"Well that's one of the problems. I don't know for sure."

Recker looked confused as he took the phone from his ear and held it in front of his face as he stared at it. "Uh, should we just start this whole conversation over again?"

"Real funny."

"No, seriously, you're telling me there's something big brewing, but you don't have details and you don't know who's involved. You're not really telling me anything."

"Well if you'd shut up for a minute and listen to me for a hot second, I might be able to tell you what I'm thinking."

"Oh, this should be good."

"You want this info or not, man?"

"I'm just riding you, go ahead."

"OK, so I don't have specific names or anything, but from what I can tell, everything's revolving around that new woman, what's her name... Nowak?"

"Yeah. What makes you think it's her?"

"Because I know some people that have been working for her. Not on her payroll or nothing, but she hired some dudes for scouting missions, going deep into Vincent's territory and all."

"What for?" Recker asked.

"Don't know. They came back to her with where his men liked to go, how many usually went to certain places, time of day, things like that."

"Could be she's just keeping an eye on them."

"Yeah, I don't think so, man. I know some of the guys she hired, apparently they didn't want to use Nowak's associated men because they didn't want Vincent's crew to spot them. She's trying to sneak in all quiet and stuff."

"She's already started something with Vincent," Recker said. "I really doubt she's gonna be able to sneak up on him again."

"Maybe. That don't mean she won't try though."

"So'd you tell Vincent all this?"

"What do you think I am?"

Recker laughed. "I know what you are."

"What's that supposed to mean?"

"It means you already have a good relationship with him. Figure you telling me that kind of information would be worth something. And I've never known you to pass down a buck."

"Yeah, well, maybe I slipped a piece of paper to him or something."

Recker laughed again. "See? I know you."

"Yeah, yeah, well, since his business has a way of becoming your business, I just figured I'd give you a heads up too, just in case you get drawn into it somehow."

"Thanks for the heads up."

After hanging up, Recker let the others know the gist of the conversation with Tyrell.

"I have a feeling she's not gonna go away anytime soon," Haley said.

"I would agree," Jones replied. "I believe she might wind up being a more formidable foe than either Jeremiah or the Italians for Vincent."

"Well if you recall, Vincent didn't take either of those out."

"I'm painfully aware. Can I please make a suggestion and sit this one out, please?"

"You know me," Recker said with a smile. "I just go where the crime takes me."

Jones gave him an eye roll and went back to his work. Recker and Haley went back to their relaxation techniques. About twenty minutes quietly went by before one of Jones' computers started beeping. They all knew what that meant. Recker and Haley quickly sat up at attention, wondering what had happened. That beep always meant something unexpected had happened. Something big.

"Holy Hannah," Jones marveled, looking at the screen.

Recker and Haley looked at each other, then jumped off the couch and moved in behind Jones.

"What is it?" Recker asked.

"An explosion."

"Where?"

"Some trucking facility." Jones started typing, bringing up the address on screen.

"I know that place."

Jones then brought up a picture of the building on the larger screen. "Isn't that?"

Recker nodded. "Yeah. That's Vincent's place. The one that he brought me to all those times."

"I wonder what happened?" Haley asked.

"I don't think you need to wonder long."

"Nowak?"

"Yeah. This has gotta be her doing. Tyrell said she had people scouting. This is probably step one."

"I don't really get it though. I mean, if you're after Vincent, and you wanna take him by surprise, this isn't really gonna help. It's just gonna put him on high alert. If you wanna take him out, you gotta make that your first action. Everything after this just makes that task harder."

"I would assume she knows that," Recker said. "This isn't about taking him out. This is about sending a message."

"I just think that's stupid. Vincent's not gonna scare. He's not some two-bit punk who's just getting his feet wet and will run at the first sign of trouble. He's gonna bunker down and fight back."

"Maybe that's what she's counting on," Jones said. "Maybe she doesn't think she can get Vincent. At least not at first. Maybe this is her saying I'm going to take out everything around you first and leave you as the last man standing. At that point he would have nothing left to fight with."

Recker shook his head, knowing none of their theories would be pleasant. "This is gonna be a long and violent war."

"And a public one at that," Haley said.

"Question is how many innocent people are gonna get hurt by them in the process?"

"We are not getting involved in it though, correct?" Jones asked.

"We're not?"

"We have gotten involved in Vincent's business all too often over the years. Some of it has been necessary, no doubt. But at times we have gotten involved when it wasn't necessary. When we've had other options."

"I don't really agree."

"Even so, this thing they have going on does not concern us."

"Until the first innocent victim drops. Then it will concern us."

Jones sternly looked at him, not wanting to get into another one of their differences of opinion. "Michael, this is between two criminal parties and we will stay out of it. Like you have always suggested. Vincent has manipulated us, and you in particular, far too often over the years in order to get you to do his dirty work so he can have more power and influence. You're not going to make his job and life easier for him again."

"I thought our position here was to protect innocent people from getting hurt?"

"Yes, well, that has not happened yet has it?"

"Well, when it does?"

"Then we will talk about it at that time."

"OK," Recker agreed. "We'll stay out of it for now. But if innocent people start getting killed, I'm gonna make it my business."

**4**

———

Recker knew what he wanted. As soon as he saw the caller ID on his phone, he knew what it was about. Ever since the explosion happened the day before, he'd been waiting for this call. He didn't think for a second that Vincent wouldn't reach out to him. When his phone started ringing, Jones looked over at him, and from the look on Recker's face, he knew who was calling as well. Just as he was about to answer, Jones had some last-minute advice.

"Don't get suckered into anything," Jones said.

Recker glared at him and shrugged it off, not paying him much attention. "Hey," Recker greeted.

"I have something to discuss with you," Vincent said. "Are you available at some point today?"

"Uh, I don't know, I'm kind of busy."

"I'm only asking for a few minutes."

"Where?"

"Same diner as usual. An hour from now?"

"What's it about?" Recker asked, not wanting to travel just to turn Vincent down in his request for help.

"You know I don't like to discuss things over the phone."

Recker sighed, knowing he was going to have to go. Though he assumed what it was about, there was always a slight possibility it involved something else. He'd hate to blow off the meeting if there was something else important that might have involved him.

"One hour?"

"One hour."

After hanging up, Recker could feel Jones' icy stare without even looking at him. He knew Jones was giving him a disapproving look. Recker stared at his phone for a minute before finally glancing up at his partner. He was correct in his assumption.

"Don't look at me like that," Recker said.

"I'm not saying anything."

"It's not what you're saying, it's what you're thinking."

"I'm not thinking anything."

"Don't give me that. I know you know that was Vincent and I know you know he asked for a meeting and I know you don't want me to attend."

"I would say you have everything well covered," Jones replied.

"I'm just going to listen to what he has to say in case it's something else. I promise I won't get us involved in something that's not our business."

Jones pulled open a few drawers and pretended to be rummaging for something. "Wait, will you put your hand on a Bible and swear to it?"

"Really? We both know you don't keep a Bible in there."

"Well how about if I print out a picture of it and we use that?"

"I give you my word."

"I guess that will have to do."

"Need me to come with?" Haley asked.

"Nah. Stay here in case something else breaks. I won't be too long."

Recker made sure his firearms were loaded, then headed out of the office for his meeting. He wound up getting to the diner about twenty minutes ahead of schedule. Vincent was already there, evidenced by one of his bodyguards at the door. After a brief greeting with the man, Recker went inside, immediately acknowledged by Malloy. They gave each other a nod, which seemed to be their usual greeting, a sign of mutual respect between the two.

"How ya moving these days?" Recker asked, his eyes moving down to Malloy's midsection, where he was previously shot.

"Almost back to normal."

"So, I probably shouldn't give you a good rib shot right now?"

Malloy grinned. "Not if you wanna walk out of here." Recker looked to the back of the diner and saw Vincent sitting there. "You're a little early."

"You know me, no use putting off for later what you can do now. He ready?"

"Yeah, go ahead."

Vincent had been reading a newspaper but folded it up and put it to the side when he saw Recker approaching. He got up and gave his frequent business associate a handshake before they sat down across from each other.

"Thank you for coming on such short notice," Vincent said. "Hopefully, I didn't pull you away from anything urgent."

"Nothing that couldn't wait. So, what's this about?"

"As I'm sure you know and have heard by now, one of my properties was hit with an explosive yesterday."

"Yeah, I'll miss conducting business there," Recker deadpanned.

"Be that as it may, we both know who was behind it."

"Nowak."

"Exactly. I have a proposition for you."

Recker, having an idea what he was about to say, wanted to stop it before he even started. He put his hand up to prevent Vincent from going any further. "Before you say anything, whatever's going on between you two is between you two. It's not my fight."

"I had a feeling you would say that. I'm sure David would be proud of you for that also since I'm sure that's his feeling as well."

"We've got our own things to work on right now. We just can't intervene in this."

"What if I made it worth your while to assist me in this quest to rid the city of these scoundrels?"

"No amount of money will persuade us," Recker answered. "You should know that by now."

"I wasn't referring to money. You can name your price. Whatever you want."

Though Recker was a little bowled over by the offer, he wasn't even sure how to respond. As big an offer as it was, Recker wouldn't know what to even ask for. He shook his head slightly as he tried to think of something, not that he was seriously entertaining the offer, no matter how appealing it was. Seeing that his proposition was falling on deaf ears, Vincent was willing to do whatever he could to enlist the services of Recker and his partners.

"You have a blank check. You can write in what you wish."

Recker continued to shake his head, refusing to let himself get roped in to another one of Vincent's causes. "No, I just can't do it. Not right now."

"What would be the reason for that?"

"Like I said, we just have our own things to work on right now."

"I noticed you didn't say never somewhere in there," Vincent said, still holding on to the hope of being assisted by The Silencer's crew.

"Never know what might happen down the line. But it can't happen at this moment."

"Is that your final answer?"

"I'm afraid that it is."

Vincent leaned forward, speaking more softly. "I can respect your position, whether I agree with it or not. But you've kind of positioned yourself as a man of the people.

Protecting those who can't or won't protect themselves. I'm sure you are as aware of this as I am... if Nowak and I get into the war that she seems to crave... and that I'm almost obligated to respond to, there's going to be a lot of innocent lives lost."

"You don't have to respond in the same manner."

Vincent glanced over Recker's shoulder, not looking at anything in particular, making a face like he wasn't sure whether he agreed with Recker's assessment. "Well, that's probably a matter that could be debated. But if I let her get away with this without a public and violent response in the same manner, then I am saying to everyone in this city that I am weak and vulnerable to others doing the same."

"You could operate in stealth."

"I could. But that doesn't have quite the same sting to it. We both know how this game works. If this conflict between us goes on for any length of time, innocent people will be killed. It's inevitable."

"So, make it not so."

"All I can do is try to prevent it on my end."

"I would like to think that our relationship is way beyond making idle threats or warnings."

"I would agree."

"But if innocent people get caught up in this... I will get involved. And I can't guarantee I'm coming in on a certain side. I'll come in on the side of the people. And whoever's on the wrong side of that will be lining up against me."

Vincent nodded, knowing that his plan of getting Recker on his side in this conflict wasn't working. "Understood."

**5**

———

Several days had passed since Recker's meeting with Vincent and not another incident had cropped up. It was quiet. Almost too quiet for Recker's tastes. Though some in the office, Jones in particular, held out hope that it meant that Vincent took Recker's talk to heart, that there would be no violent and public response to Nowak's actions, Recker did not share those beliefs. In his mind, it just meant that the response would be even greater, with Vincent taking extra time and precaution to get all the details right.

Recker had just finished having dinner with Mia at the hospital since she was working a night shift. Though he was planning on going back to the office since there didn't seem to be anything pressing, his plans would soon change. As soon as he left the hospital, his phone started ringing. Since it was pouring with rain at the time, Recker waited until he got across the parking lot and into his car to answer his phone. It had stopped ringing by that time, but since he saw it was Tyrell on the call log, immediately called him back.

"Hey, saw you called. What's up?"

"Hey, just wanted to give you a heads up if you want it."

"On what?" Recker asked.

"Yo, I just heard from a dude that there is something major going down in back of a jewelry shop on seventeenth. You know the place?"

"Yeah, I think I've passed by there before. What's the deal?"

"I don't know, man. All I heard is it is m-a-j-o-r."

"That doesn't really tell me much."

"All I can do is tell you what I know," Tyrell replied.

"What time's this supposed to be happening?"

"Like in thirty minutes."

"Nothing like advance notice, huh?"

"All I can do is report it when I hear it."

"OK, thanks. I'll check it out."

"Hey, wait a minute. I haven't even told you the best part yet."

"Oh. You got more?"

"Yeah, man. I hear that Nowak is connected to this."

"Why?"

"I dunno, man, that's your department."

"Why would she need to knock over a jewelry store?" Recker asked.

"Hey, I didn't say anything about it getting knocked over. Could be anything. Maybe it's just some kind of meeting, maybe they're meeting with another guy, maybe they need more money, heck... maybe the woman wants some more jewelry without having to dish out the cash for it. I'm just telling you what I know."

Though Recker was grateful for the tip, something didn't seem right about it. Though by now he had no concerns or worries about Tyrell's honesty or loyalty, Recker was still apprehensive about how he obtained this kind of information.

"Where'd you get this from?"

"Just a guy I know."

"Use him before?" Recker asked.

"Yeah, bunch of times."

"He reliable?"

"Always has been before."

"Where would he get it?"

"I dunno, man, he runs around certain circles. He's like a fly on the wall sometimes."

"You trust him?"

"Like I said, he's never let me down before. Could he be mistaken? Maybe. Is he flat out lying? Don't know why he would be, but hey, there's always a first time for everything. I just pass the info along to you. Whether you wanna act on it or not is your business."

"That's all there is to it?"

"That's it." Recker was silent for a minute, prompting Tyrell to wonder what was wrong. "What's bugging you about this? Why you trippin'?"

"I just don't see what Nowak would be doing having a meeting in the pouring rain behind a jewelry store."

"Well I didn't say it was her. Maybe it's just one of her peeps or something, you know."

"Yeah, maybe. How much did you pay for this info?"

"Didn't cost me a dime, man."

"Isn't that kind of unusual?"

"Yeah, a little."

"You mean, this guy just called you up out of the blue and told you all of this without expecting anything back?"

"Uh, yeah, kinda something like that. He did tell me that I might owe him one somewhere down the line if it played out."

"All right, I'll check it out."

"You got it. Listen, if you really wigged out about this, you make sure you watch your back out there. Don't go out there playing hero, you got me?"

"I got you."

"Aright. There's always another day."

"Let's hope so."

As soon as he got off the phone with Tyrell, Recker called Jones to let him know of the developments. As much as Recker's alarm bells went off, it was tenfold with Jones. He wanted Recker to skip the whole thing.

"I don't like it," Jones said.

"Neither do I. But that's the business we're in, isn't it? It's not all gonna be peaches and cream."

"But it also shouldn't be kale and sauerkraut either."

"Huh?"

"Forget it. The point is that we need more time to digest this."

"David, there isn't time. This thing's going down soon."

"But we also agreed not to intervene in Vincent and Nowak's feud."

"Yes, but it's the same deal I always told Vincent. I don't want to get involved in a criminal versus criminal thing, but if it involves innocent people, I can't stay away. And it might not even involve her. Maybe one of her underlings is planning to knock the place over. Aren't we supposed to act on that? Isn't that what we signed up for? Sometimes things happen at a moment's notice and we gotta roll on it. Won't be the first time."

"Yes, but that doesn't make me have to like it any better."

"I'll be careful."

"I'll have Chris meet you there."

"How far away is he?"

"He's here at the office with me. I'll have him go now."

After getting off the phone with Jones, Recker just sat in the driver's seat of his car, staring out the rain-soaked windshield. As the rain pelted the glass, Recker's mind took him elsewhere. He thought about the alley behind the jewelry store, visualizing it in his mind. He placed himself there, moving about the shadows through the darkened alley. Recker's thoughts then turned to one of his dreams, the one in which he was gunned down, killed in a similar scenario. It was the same set of circumstances. A dark alley late at night, a blistering rain, a dangerous situation.

For the first time he could ever think of, Recker thought of not rolling on the call. The prospect of his dream actually becoming a reality gave him cause for concern. A couple minutes went by, but he couldn't in good conscience not check it out. Regardless of his feelings, or whatever worries he had, he couldn't just ignore it. If he chose to let it go, and he later found out someone innocent had gotten hurt, he wouldn't be able to forgive himself. He couldn't sit this one out.

Recker started the car and put it in drive, knowing he didn't have time to waste. He was already a few minutes behind schedule after daydreaming. He put his foot on the gas to make sure he got there in good time, though knowing he couldn't push it too fast with the slick roads. Still, he got to 17th street only a minute or two after the scheduled time that Tyrell told him. He first drove along the street, passing the jewelry store to see if he could see anything going down from the front of it. Everything seemed quiet though. He continued driving, making the first turn possible, stopping near the alleyway entrance to see if he could make anything out. It was still quiet.

Though the alley was big enough for his car to drive down, it was just barely large enough, and Recker worried about getting trapped in there with no place to go, and no way to escape. The jewelry store was also near the middle of the street, flanked by a bunch of other buildings on both sides. Recker was going to have to park somewhere and go the rest of the way on foot.

Recker finally parked on the next street over so he could double back. He got out of his car and started walking but stopped just beyond the bumper. Those unpleasant thoughts came rushing back to him as the rain battered his face, his hair quickly becoming soaked by the onslaught of water. He turned around and looked at the trunk of his car and then opened it. As the trunk opened, he stared at the bullet-proof vest that was lying by his black bag of weapons. He almost always carried the vest with him, but yet seldomly used it. Most of the time he liked to move quickly into a situation and didn't have time to throw one on, though he knew he should have used it more often than he did. This would be one of those times he figured it was a good idea. He quickly grabbed the vest and put it on, closing his trunk as he then ventured toward the jewelry store.

With the rain driving down, Recker thought of how much he hated being out in weather like this. Visibility was always a concern, as was traction on the ground, not to mention losing grip on his weapon, possibly when he needed it the most. Recker navigated through some tight spaces between buildings as he made his way to the alley. After only a few minutes, his clothes were saturated, feeling like he'd just been submerged in a pool with his clothes on.

After successfully maneuvering to the alley behind the jewelry store, he was still several buildings away from the location. He clung to a wall behind a green dumpster that was overflowing with trash, pools of water forming underneath his feet. He stood there frozen, patiently watching and waiting for any sign of life being out there other than himself. He suddenly felt the vibration of his phone going off in his pocket, an incoming text message from Haley, letting his partner know he was about ten minutes away.

A few minutes later, a bright light shone across Recker's face, but only for a fleeting second. He quickly looked to his left and saw an incoming truck. It looked to be some kind of van, unmarked, its headlights lighting up the alleyway as Recker ducked down behind the dumpster as the van passed his location. It went further down, well past Recker's position, not stopping until it was directly behind the jewelry store.

Recker kept still, peering around the edge of the dumpster as he tried to figure out what was going on. About ten seconds after the van stopped, the doors opened and four guys jumped out of it, heading for the back door of the store. The back door suddenly opened, allowing the men to come inside.

"Well that's interesting," Recker said to himself. "Inside job."

Recker couldn't tell if there was anyone remaining inside the van, but his instincts told him there was. There was usually always a guy on the outside being used as a lookout. Recker finally broke from his position but had to tread carefully to avoid being spotted by someone that he couldn't see. The hard rain and murkiness of the night definitely helped to conceal his movements. He tried to stay as close to the brick wall as possible and tried to move slowly so he didn't alert anyone by hearing the splashing water that would kick up into the air from his feet.

Recker continued to inch closer to the van as the rain came down even harder if that were possible. At least it wasn't windy though, as that would have made it nightmarish conditions. Recker wanted to get to the van before the men came back out, since he didn't envy going up against four men at the same time. At least if he could get to the van, he could catch them by surprise, and cut down their numbers at the same time. But he knew he needed to move faster than he was. The men weren't going to take their time and stay inside the store forever, assuming they were there to rob the place. If they weren't there for that and were having some kind of high-level meeting, Recker would have more time. But he couldn't count on that. And considering he couldn't even make out any of the men that went inside the building, he had no way of knowing. He had to go with the assumption that they were picking the place clean.

After taking a few minutes to get to the van, Recker was finally ready to make his move. He was only a few feet away from it. With his back against the wall, he took one last look around and took a deep breath. With the coast seemingly clear, he took a step toward the van. Suddenly, both the back and side doors opened up, with a man stepping out from both spots. Recker knew he was in a jam now.

Recker quickly lifted his arm, taking aim at the man who stepped out of the side door. He didn't get a chance to pull the trigger though. The man at the back of the van, who spotted Recker approaching several minutes earlier, was just a tad faster, and more ready for the action. The man fired two shots, both of which hit Recker in the chest. The impacts of the blasts knocked Recker off his feet. The man at the side of the door also fired a couple rounds, but his shots missed since Recker was falling backwards. Recker's gun flew out of his hand before he hit the puddle-filled concrete ground, the back of his head smacking the concrete.

Hearing the shots outside, the back door to the jewelry store pushed open, the men filing outside to see what the commotion was.

"What's going on?" one of the men asked.

"Found this guy sneaking up on us," the man that shot Recker answered.

The men walked over to the van and put several bags inside of it, presumably their haul from the store. "Well finish him and let's go."

The man walked over to Recker, who was completely out of it. Between the shock of getting shot, and his head bouncing off the concrete like a basketball, he was in a world of hurt. The man wiped off his gun by placing it between his arm and his side before pointing it at Recker's head. Another shot rang out. The man dropped like a lead sack, falling just in front of Recker's prone position.

"What was that?" one of the men asked.

"Where'd that come from?" another one said.

"Over there, over there!" several said in unison as they spotted a man approaching from the end of the alley.

Another shot rang out, hitting the back of the van and glancing off.

"Just get in, let's go!"

The group, not wanting to get into a firefight in the middle of an alley, just wanted to get out of there. They'd already gotten what they came for. There was no need to engage.

"What about Bobby?!" a man asked, hopping into the van.

"He's already gone. Nothing we can do for him now," the leader replied, getting in the front passenger seat.

The van sped off, squealing its tires off the slickened ground. As it drove off, Haley sprinted down the alley until he got to Recker's motionless body.

"You all right, you all right?!" Haley asked, kneeling next to his friend as he checked on his condition.

Recker didn't move a muscle as Haley looked on in horror, terrified by the fate of his partner. Haley grabbed Recker's hand, then placed his other hand behind his friend's head, lifting it up slightly off the ground, trying to get some kind of sign that he was OK. As he did, Haley noticed a little bit of blood on the ends of his fingers from touching the back of Recker's head. Finally, after what was the longest twenty seconds of Haley's life, Recker twitched. He let out a small groan, moved his arm, and batted his eyes. Haley felt a slight sense of relief, hoping nothing was fatally wrong.

"You OK?" Haley asked.

Recker tried sitting up, needing his friend's help in doing so. He took a few deep breaths as he put his right hand on his chest, clutching his vest. As he was catching his breath, Haley leaned over to take a peek at the back of Recker's head, observing the damage back there.

"Thank God for these vests," Recker said.

"You hit?"

Recker shook his head. "Think the vest stopped both of them." He then put his hand on the back of his head to try to stop the throbbing pain. It felt like someone was continuously hitting him with a hammer.

"We're gonna have to get out of here before the cops show up," Haley said.

"Yeah."

Recker said it in a way that indicated he wasn't moving anywhere. At least not quickly.

"C'mon, we gotta go."

Haley grabbed hold of Recker's arm and helped lift him off the ground. Recker put his arm around Haley's shoulder, needing help in walking. The two of them walked back down to the end of the alley until they got to Haley's car, which he parked crooked, halfway on a side-walk, knowing he was arriving late to the party. Once they got to Haley's vehicle, he helped Recker get into the back seat so he could stretch out.

As soon as Haley started the car back up and got on the road, he started evaluating Recker's condition more closely. "Anything else wrong with you beside your head?"

"You mean that and feeling like an elephant stomped on my chest?"

"Yeah."

"Isn't that enough?"

"Looks like you took a good whack on the back of your head there."

"Yeah."

"Might need to get you checked out," Haley said. "You might have a concussion."

"I'm fine."

"You know what today is?"

"Of course I do."

"What day is it?"

"Uh," Recker suddenly struggled to remember, his mind feeling foggy. "It's... Tuesday."

Haley raised his eyebrows and looked at him through the rearview mirror. "Uh, yeah, I think we're gonna need Mia."

**6**

———

Haley drove straight to the office, letting Jones know he was coming with a wounded Recker in tow. Wanting to concentrate on the hazardous conditions while driving, Haley didn't say much about Recker's condition. He just texted Jones that their friend was hurt, but it wasn't life threatening. Since getting Haley's message, Jones couldn't concentrate on anything else and just stood by the window, waiting with bated breath as he looked down at the parking lot.

Once Jones finally saw the headlights of Haley's car pull into the lot, he anxiously tried to look through the raindrops that saturated the window. He saw Haley helping Recker out of the car and putting his arm around him to assist him in walking. Jones hurried over to the door and opened it, waiting for their appearance. Once they appeared from the side of the building and started walking up the steps, Jones wanted to run down and help Recker up, but two people fitting side by side up the steps was a challenge, three would have been impossible.

Both Recker and Haley were completely soaked from the rain, head to toe. Once they got to the top of the steps and inside the office, Haley led Recker over to the couch. Recker still had his vest off, which his friends helped get off him. Recker was still holding the back of his head, so Jones took a closer look at it.

"I think we're going to need Mia," Jones said. "This cut looks pretty bad. Might need a stitch or two."

"That's not all," Haley said.

"What do you mean?" Jones' eyes darted all around Recker's body, looking for a bullet hole. "Has he been shot?"

"Well, yeah, but the vest caught those."

"Those?"

"Yeah, two of them."

"What else is the issue?"

"He's a little hazy about things," Haley answered. "He has no idea what day we're in."

"Sustained a concussion most likely."

"Yeah, that's what I figured."

"We're still going to need Mia," Jones said. "Mike, is Mia at work tonight or is she home?"

Recker's eyes looked glossy. He tried to remember, but for some reason, it just wasn't coming back to him. Jones could see that he wasn't going to get an answer out of him in his current condition. It was best to just let him relax and not put any strain on him.

"I believe Mike told me earlier that she's working a night shift tonight."

"I can go get here," Haley said. "Probably not best for her to be out driving in this and worried about him at the same time."

"Yes, good idea. You get started for the hospital and I'll call her to let her know you're coming."

After Haley left, Jones went and got some aspirin and a cup of water for his friend. "Here, this might help with the headache."

Recker took them from Jones' hand and quickly gulped them down before leaning back on the couch. Recker looked up at the lights and squinted. Jones knew the lights being on wasn't helping, so he turned them all off, except for a small lamp on the desk and a table lamp in the far corner of the room. Knowing Mia kept her phone on her at all times, Jones sent her a message to call her as soon as possible.

*"Please call me as soon as possible,"* the message read.

Jones expected a call back in about thirty seconds, but it actually took a few minutes longer than that. But it still came as he expected it would. As soon as he heard Mia's voice, he could tell she was automatically worried.

"First of all, calm down, everything is fine."

"Everything's fine? I know that's not true. You wouldn't be calling me if it was."

"I'm actually surprised it took you five minutes to call me back."

"Well I was helping a new mother at the time. Now what is it? Is Mike hurt? Is he OK? What's the matter?"

Jones hesitated for not even five seconds, which was almost enough to send Mia over the brink. "David, don't play around with me, what is it? He's hurt, isn't he? Is he shot? I knew something like this was coming."

"OK, just relax."

"David, you tell me to calm down and relax one more time without telling me what's wrong I'm gonna come over there and shove something completely inappropriate up your..."

"OK, OK, message received. Mike is injured, but he's OK, he's not..."

"Oh my god, what's wrong? What happened?"

"Calm... I mean, just let me explain."

"Well hurry up and do it fast," Mia replied.

"OK, Mike got caught up in a situation where..."

"David, I really don't care about the situation, I just wanna know how Mike is right now."

"He's OK. Resting on the couch, a few bumps and bruises, but basically OK."

"What does that mean exactly? What are his symptoms?"

"Well, we believe he has a concussion."

"Oh...," Mia said, not even finishing her sentence as she ran her hand through her long jet-black hair. "What was he struck with?"

"Nothing. He smacked the back of his head on the concrete. I'm not sure if he ever lost consciousness or not, Chris didn't say."

"Chris was with him?"

"At the end of it."

Mia couldn't shake the feeling that there was something that Jones was holding back. "Is there something you're not telling me?"

"Well…"

"There is. Spill it."

"Umm, well, he apparently was also shot…"

"Oh, my god. No."

"Mia, he was wearing a vest. Nothing penetrated, he's OK, the vest stopped both bullets."

"Two? Oh my…"

"Mia, he's basically OK from that. His only worries right now are the back of his head, which is still bleeding, and what I believe to be a concussion."

"Well, I need to come see him and make sure he's OK."

"I already figured as much. Chris is already on his way to pick you up and bring you here."

"I don't wanna wait for him. I need to leave now."

"Mia, it's almost hurricane-like rain out there, I don't want you driving in it while you're also worrying about Michael. Just wait for Chris to get there so he can do the driving. Please."

Mia let out a deep and audible sigh. "OK. You're sure he doesn't have any bullet holes in him?"

"Well I mean, I could strip all his clothes off to inspect him further, but there's no blood stains that would suggest it. Not to mention both he and Chris said the only thing wrong with him was his head."

"Don't get smart, David."

"I'm sorry, I know this is terrifying for you, but I promise, he's going to be OK. When can you be ready to leave?"

"Oh, thanks for reminding me about that. I have to go tell them I have to go."

"Is that going to be a problem for you?"

"No, I'll just tell them it's an emergency, it's fine. When is Chris gonna get here?"

"Uh, probably should be about ten or fifteen minutes I would say."

"OK, I gotta go then," Mia replied. "I'll see you when I get there. I gotta pack up and leave, then I'll wait down in the lobby for Chris."

Mia asked for and was granted permission to leave for an emergency, then quickly got her things together. She hurried down to the lobby of the hospital and waited outside, underneath a covered portion of the entrance. She didn't even care about the rain at that point. She barely noticed it. All she could think about was Recker's condition.

Even though Mia knew that her boyfriend was going to be alright, that didn't stop all the bad thoughts going on inside her head. If it was only a concussion as Jones explained, even as bad as that was, at least he was still alive. But for how much longer? Maybe this was the sign that Recker needed to get out, she thought. Between the nightmares he'd been having, now almost living them out, not to mention the fact that he'd been shot before. Her heart was feeling heavy thinking about how different the outcome tonight could have been. What if he hadn't been wearing that bullet-proof vest, which she knew he didn't often wear? She could barely stomach the thought.

About twenty minutes after Jones' call, Haley pulled

up to the hospital entrance. Mia ran toward the car, not at all caring about the driving rain. Her only concern was getting to Recker as soon as possible. She put her backpack on the floor between her legs, then leaned over and gave Haley a hug, squeezing him hard.

"It's OK," Haley said. "He's going to be fine."

"Yeah, this time."

"It's just a concussion and a nasty cut. He'll be up and around in no time."

Mia finally let go of him and wiped her nose and eyes, not wanting to break down. Haley grabbed her hand.

"He's going to be OK."

Mia smiled at him, but it wasn't one of her warm smiles that lit up a room. It was a forced one that suggested she didn't believe it. "Yeah."

Haley started driving, trying to talk to Mia along the way to relieve the stress that she was obviously feeling. Nothing he said seemed to work very well.

"What happens next time?" Mia asked. "What happens next time if he isn't so lucky?"

"Mia, you can't think like that."

"But I have to. It's a very real possibility. Every time you guys go out, there's a chance you won't be coming back."

It was getting a little deeper than Haley was comfortable with, but it didn't seem like he could really avoid it. "You just have to trust that we know what we're doing and we're not gonna put ourselves in bad situations."

"But that's the job. All you guys do is put yourself in bad situations. Every single time. I mean, that's the life."

"I know."

"I mean, yeah he just has a concussion right now, but it could have been a lot worse. He could have a couple holes in him right now that I'd have to dig out of him."

"But he doesn't."

"That's not the point. The point is, he was really close tonight. If he wasn't wearing that vest, we might not even be having this conversation."

Haley sighed, knowing he probably wasn't going to win this conversation. All he could do was try to diffuse her anger a little bit. He couldn't really argue against anything she was saying as it was all technically true, but he didn't want to be the one talking to her about the dangers of their work. That was Recker's job. All he wanted to do was try to calm her down.

As they continued to drive, Mia started to stare out the window. Haley tried talking to her some more, but she wasn't responding. She wasn't really there. Her mind was thinking back to some of the mornings she observed Recker waking up from one of his nightmares. Then she thought of their conversation at breakfast a few days prior to that.

"You OK?" Haley asked, looking over, trying to get her attention.

Mia finally snapped out of her funk and looked at him. "Hmm?"

"You all right? Seemed like you were out of it or something."

"Oh. No, I'm fine."

"Doesn't seem like it."

"No, I was just thinking of something."

"Wanna share?"

Mia looked at him and wanted to talk about it but wasn't sure that she should. She didn't think that Recker would want her talking to anyone about it, especially Haley or Jones. Recker never wanted to appear vulnerable about anything, and Mia had to respect his wishes.

"I can't really talk about it."

"You sure?" Haley asked. It sounded to him like one of those things that people say they don't want to talk about, but really do, and just need a push to get started. "I'm here if you wanna share."

Mia thought about it for another minute, trying to figure out how she could rephrase it, so it didn't sound like it was Recker's problem. "Do you ever have dreams about you... getting killed?"

Haley tilted his head to the side. "Wow. That's kind of a weird question."

"But do you?"

"Not that I can recall. If I have, it wasn't something that I remembered when I woke up."

"Oh." Mia was somewhat disappointed. Not that she wished Haley to be having nightmares, but if he did, she would take some comfort in knowing it wasn't just Recker. Maybe it would kind of be something that just happened with the job.

"Why?" Haley asked.

"Uh... it's just lately, I've been having these dreams, nightmares about Mike getting killed doing various things. Sometimes it's even been you, David, and even me."

"You have, huh?"

"Yeah."

"You've been having dreams like this?" Haley was getting the feeling that she was actually speaking for someone else and just changing the names around.

"Is that surprising?"

"A little. I would have thought Mike would have mentioned it before now."

"You know how he is. Stubborn. Doesn't like to admit problems."

"Kind of like some other people I know," Haley said, looking over at her.

"So, what do you think this dream problem of mine is?"

"Is it really giving you a lot of problems?"

"Yeah, sometimes. I mean it's almost like every night now. Sometimes he... I wake up sweating and it's just disturbing sometimes."

"What does Mike say?"

"Oh. Uh, he just tries to play it off like they're just dreams, nothing more."

"Maybe that's all it is," Haley said.

"But one of the dreams was Mike getting killed in an alley late at night and now..."

"Mia, I don't believe that having a dream is a precursor to something becoming a reality. I think it's more along the lines of something really being on a person's brain, stressing them out, worrying them constantly, and then while they're sleeping, they can't shut that part of their mind off, so what's been bothering them becomes a dream."

"I guess that makes sense."

"At least that's how I rationalize it. Don't know if that's technically correct or not, but that's how I see it."

"But what if he becomes more hesitant because of them? Afraid that they might come true."

"Why would he become hesitant over your dreams? Especially if he doesn't know the details."

"Oh," Mia said, embarrassed that she'd even suggest it. "You're right. That's silly of me to even think it."

Haley thought about pressing her further on it, maybe even getting her to admit that it was actually Recker who was having the nightmares, but he thought better of it. It wasn't his position to drag the truth out of her if she or Recker wasn't ready to divulge it. He already knew Mia was covering for Recker anyway, so it didn't really change anything.

Once they got to the office and parked, Mia jumped out of the car and sprinted toward the back of the laundromat building. Haley couldn't even keep up with her. She then dashed up the steps and tried to enter the office, but it was locked. She started banging on the door, getting Jones' attention, and having him come over to unlock it.

"You didn't have to..."

Mia wasn't particularly interested in anything Jones had to say at the moment and raced past him as soon as the door opened.

Jones watched her rush across the room until she got

to Recker on the couch. "Well, come in," Jones said, stretching his arms out to mimic welcoming her. He then wondered where Haley was and looked down, seeing him walk up the steps. "I see you didn't have much luck in calming her down on the way over."

Haley laughed. "Are you kidding? I thought she was going to get her cape out and fly over here."

"I certainly wouldn't put it past her."

As they were talking, Mia was embracing Recker, thankful that he was still in one piece. While she was giving him affection, Jones and Haley came up behind her.

"As you can see, just like we told you, all is well and good," Jones said.

"Having a concussion and a gash on your head is not well and good," Mia replied.

She started digging through her bag and took out some medical supplies that she needed to fix Recker up. As she started working on him, Jones and Haley sat down at the desk to get out of the way.

"Does he need stitches?" Haley asked.

"Yeah," Mia answered.

Luckily, she spent time in the emergency room, where she was able to practice some of the things that she hoped she'd never have to put into use again. After putting five stitches in the back of Recker's head, she put a bandage on it. She then started to examine him to see if he had a concussion. After running some tests, flicking the lights on and off, examining his eyes, Mia was almost certain that he did indeed have a concussion. The lights bothered him, his memory was hazy, his speech was a little slurred, he had a massive headache, there was a slight ringing in his ears, he was tired, and he appeared to be dazed. All the signs were there.

"So, what do you think?" Jones asked. "Does he have a concussion?"

"Oh, yeah," Mia replied.

"You're certain?"

"Well, I can't say a hundred percent since the only way to officially diagnose it is lab tests or a scan, but he's got every symptom, so I'm ninety-nine percent confident that he does have one."

"So, what is your prognosis?"

"He needs rest. That's it. There's no pill or medicine that will make it go away. He just needs to rest."

"For how long?"

Mia sighed. "Tough to say. There's no way of telling for sure. He just needs to go home and rest. Could be a day or two. Could be a week or two. Every concussion is different, and everyone reacts to them differently. It also could depend on how many previous concussions he's had as they usually get worse the more you have."

"Well, that's not good," Haley said.

"Yeah, and I have a sneaky suspicion that, considering who we're talking about, this isn't his first one."

"It'd be a miracle if it was," Jones replied.

"Yeah. So, right now, he just needs to go home and rest for a few days."

"And what if he wakes up tomorrow and says he's ready to go?"

"David?"

Jones put his hands up, not wanting to get into a fight with her. "I'm not arguing with you. He can take as much time as he needs. I'm just saying... we all know him. And he's going to try to come back probably sooner than he's actually ready."

"I will take care of that."

"How do you propose to manage that? How are you going to keep him there? Put him in handcuffs?"

A wicked smile came over Mia's face. "That's a pleasant thought, isn't it?"

"I... I don't want to know. Forget I said anything."

"Uh, should he be doing that?" Haley asked, pointing at Recker falling asleep on the couch.

"Yeah, why not?" Mia said.

"I thought you were supposed to stay awake for a while after a concussion? Is that not true?"

"Oh, no, that's a myth. The concern used to be that if you slept, you might slip into a coma or that you wouldn't wake up. But now sleep is actually encouraged and can help in the healing process. Some people find it hard to sleep after a concussion, so it's actually a good sign that he can. I'll just have to keep an eye on him, periodically check on him, ask him questions, things like that."

"I have a feeling this might be awhile," Jones said.

"Like I said, tough to say. He could be back in two days, good as new, no signs or symptoms at all. Or we could be here a week from now and he might still be suffering from light issues or dizziness. It's just impossible to say."

"Whatever the case, looks like we'll be flying short for a few days at the least," Haley said.

"It would appear so," Jones said, more concerned for his friend's health and well-being than he was at being shorthanded.

"How are we going to keep him at bay?"

"Well he can't stay here," Mia said. "You guys are working, it's hectic, things are happening, lights are on, it's gonna be hard for him to rest here. Plus, he'll want to jump right back into things if he sees you guys. I'm gonna have to take him home."

"You want me to help you get him to the apartment?" Haley asked.

"If you wouldn't mind."

"Sure."

"The bigger question is going to be keeping him there," Jones said.

"I'll take care of it," Mia replied. "I've got a few vacation days I can use, I hardly ever use sick time, plus I was off for the next three days, anyway. So, I can take the next week off if I have to. It's not a problem for me."

"He's very fortunate to have you in his life. He got lucky when he found you."

Mia smiled. "I know. Make sure you keep reminding him of it."

## 7

It'd been three days since Recker's incident in the alley behind the jewelry store. And he spent most of it either lying in bed or sleeping. Though most of the other symptoms had subsided or gone away completely, the one that remained was fatigue. He just felt very tired most of the time. Mia didn't leave his side the entire time. Both Jones and Haley dropped in to see how Recker was doing and if either he or Mia needed anything. But there was nothing they could do... nothing except wait.

Luckily the three days Recker was away so far had proved to be relatively quiet. No major incidents happened, and nothing seemed to be on the horizon. At least not that Haley could see. Jones had something different in mind. In what was kind of a departure for him, he actually was seeking out trouble. Specifically, he was looking for the men who robbed the jewelry store and shot Recker. He was trying to be proactive, considering they had a light workload at the moment, and he figured the men would eventually strike again, still putting them on their radar. Jones figured they might as well find them now and preempt any other plans the men had.

Haley walked into the office after getting a quick lunch and saw that Jones had someone's face plastered all over a couple of the computer screens. He instantly knew what he was doing. He recognized the man on the screen as the man he'd shot and killed. The one that was standing over Recker and about to do him in before Haley got there and intervened.

"What's that?" Haley asked, walking over to the desk, finishing off the last bit of his sandwich.

Jones turned his head around to look back at him for a second before continuing on with his work. "Oh, this is something I've been working on for the last few days."

"That's the guy I killed in the alley."

"Yes, I know."

"How'd you know?"

"Police records," Jones answered. "Just followed the trail. There was only one dead body recovered behind the jewelry store. It's not that hard once you know how. Just follow the trail."

"Why you looking this guy up?"

"We're in the business of stopping dangerous people from taking over this city. I would say they qualify."

"Is this because of what they did or what they did to Mike?" Haley asked.

Jones looked at him again. If it'd been anyone else, he might have gotten peeved, thinking that his integrity was being questioned. But considering who it was coming from, it didn't really bother him.

"It's a fair question I suppose," Jones said. "Maybe a little of both. But I think primarily it's because they're obviously a dangerous group that has little regret for killing anyone that stands in their way."

Haley finally took a seat next to his friend to get a better look at the information he was pulling up. "You got anything yet?"

"I've got quite a bit actually. I've been working on it for a couple days now."

"What do you have?"

"I've got a list of the most likely suspects," Jones said, handing him a piece of paper with the names. "I cross-referenced everyone with whom he was suspected of having any type of relationship, then whittled it down to these eight names."

"There weren't eight guys there though."

"I know. There were six I believe you mentioned?"

"That I can remember. Everything happened so fast. Maybe there were eight, I don't know."

"In any case, these eight men are all dangerous regardless if they were involved or not, and I suspect most of them were."

"Is there any connection to Nowak?"

"Not that I can tell."

"Nothing?" Haley asked, almost seeming disappointed.

"I have not uncovered one thing in any of their backgrounds that indicates they've ever known or met with

Nowak. Now, that doesn't mean they haven't. It just means I have not discovered it yet."

"I see."

"So, for now, any conspiracy theories about Nowak being involved or setting this up... we'll have to put them aside. So far this is lining up as just a robbery. Nothing more than that."

"What about the police? They on their trail yet?"

"Unfortunately, no," Jones replied. "Oh, they've checked on these names as well, but they've been unable at this point to locate any of them."

"They're lying low now. They're not gonna come up for air anytime soon."

"Perhaps. Perhaps not."

"You got something?"

"A woman. Sherri Bradshaw. She's a waitress at a restaurant downtown."

"What about her?"

"She's had an on-again-off-again relationship with Brad Kirby for several years now. I suspect Kirby to be the leader of this gang."

"I'm sure the cops have checked her out as well."

"They have. Unfortunately, Ms. Bradshaw has not checked in at work for the last week and hasn't been seen at her apartment in that time frame either. So, they have no idea where she is."

"Let me take a guess," Haley said. "You do."

Jones looked over at him and grinned, as if there were no need to verbally confirm it.

"So, how'd you find her?"

"The same way a lot of people get found," Jones said. "She stupidly checked into one of her social media accounts that I had taps on. From there I was able to triangulate her position and get her IP address."

"Even so, that doesn't mean she's with Kirby or any of the other ones."

"No, it does not. But it does mean there's a good chance. That's why you'll need to check it out."

"What about Kirby? Any way to trace him?"

"No," Jones said with a sigh. "He seems to be too smart to be sucked in by social media sites. He also doesn't have a traceable phone. Must be sticking with the prepaid options."

"So, where's Bradshaw at?"

Jones handed him a piece of paper with the address already written down. "Northeast. Mayfair. It's a row home that's not registered to any of the other names on the list."

"Who's it belong to?"

"A Jessie Mendoza. It's not yet clear if she has a relationship with these guys or if they're just renting the place from her."

"Could be just a rental," Haley said.

"Possible. In any case, you probably should get over there and stake the place out to see what we're dealing with."

"And when I do?"

Jones wasn't sure. He certainly wasn't eager to send Haley into a house with six or eight men ready to shoot it out with him. He didn't want to take a chance on losing Haley after narrowly averting disaster with Recker.

"I don't know," Jones said. "Let's figure out the next step after we confirm that these people are actually there."

"How close should I get?"

"Let's use our heads about this. This isn't a situation where we need to go in both guns blazing. All we need to do is get these guys off the street. If we find them all to be at this location, maybe an anonymous phone call to the police would be in order. Let them swarm in and raid them."

"You know Mike's gonna wanna get his hands on them."

"Yes, well, luckily, we're not in a position right now where we have to worry about his need for revenge, do we? Let's just see what's going on first and worry about the rest later."

Haley agreed and left soon after that, driving the half hour on Route 13 to get to his destination. Once he got there, the residence in question was a remarkably unremarkable building. Nothing different, strange, or unusual about it. It appeared to be well kept, no outward signs that would indicate a gang of violent thieves lived there. Haley parked a little down the street, about five or six houses away from the Mendoza residence. He leaned back in his seat, getting the feeling he was going to have a long night.

The next several hours went by without a single peep of activity. No one came in or out. No one walked by. Haley didn't even see a curtain in a window move as if someone was looking out. As the night wore on, he was beginning to question whether anyone was even there at all. After a couple hours of darkness, Haley called Jones to make sure they had the right place.

"You sure about this?" Haley asked.

"Positive."

"Because I haven't seen anything that makes me believe anyone's in there, let alone the people we're looking for."

"Just be patient," Jones said. "You know as well as I do that these stakeouts sometimes take a lot of time."

"I hate these. Mike's better at these than I am."

"Yes, it's somewhat strange to be honest. Under most circumstances, he's the more impatient one, yet when it comes to stakeouts, he's generally more patient than you. Quite odd."

"Tell me about it. How much longer should I give it here?"

"I would say several more hours at least. And if no one shows up, then we'll do it again tomorrow."

"Ugh. Maybe Mike's starting to rub off on me, preferring action instead of waiting around."

"There's a sobering thought," Jones said. "Let's not mention those words again. Having two of you exactly the same might be enough to drive me to start drinking."

**8**

———

Haley stayed on the house now associated with Kirby and his thugs, watching the house until two o'clock in the morning. After getting no signs of life inside, Haley went home to get a few hours of sleep, figuring he'd get an early start in the morning. He forewent his usual trek to the office, instead going back to the Mendoza house, hoping he'd get some action earlier in the day. He let Jones know what he was doing, so he didn't worry about him not showing up at the office.

Haley sat there waiting, and waiting, and waiting some more, getting extremely frustrated at the lack of progress he seemed to be achieving. He sat in his car all day, in full view of the Mendoza house, only leaving for about twenty minutes in order to grab something to eat for lunch. It was now five o'clock. Considering Jones hadn't heard from him in a while, he called Haley to ask how it was going.

"I take it from your lack of communication that there is nothing to report?"

"You said it," Haley replied.

"Hmm. Very strange."

"You're telling me. I was here all night, been here all day, and I haven't seen one person come in or out of this house."

"It could be they know they're being watched."

"They still gotta come out sometime, don't they?"

"Perhaps. Or they've got everything they need in order to stay right where they are."

"Well if that's the case, we're never gonna find anything unless I go in there."

"Let's hold off on that for a while," Jones said. "What about the back? I assume there's a back door."

"Well I'm only one person, so I can't be in two places at once."

"Let's also hold off on the sarcasm, shall we?"

"I can try to keep an eye on the back, but that's gonna be a bit trickier."

"I figured it would."

"There's a small alley between these houses and the ones behind it, enough for a car to drive through, but it's not meant for idling cars on stakeouts."

"Yes, I know, most of those alleys are only meant for owners to park their cars."

"So, the only way I'm getting back there is on foot," Haley said.

It took a few seconds for Jones to reply, wanting to avoid alleys as much as possible for the foreseeable future. "If you can do it safely. I'd like to not have any of you step foot in another alley anytime soon if we can avoid it. But it's at your discretion if you feel you can get a view."

"OK. I'll give it a shot around back."

"Just let me know how it goes."

Haley left his car parked where it was and proceeded to walk down the street and turn the corner, going into the small alleyway that was behind the houses. There were some children playing basketball on the concrete, making Haley stay on the end and not go any further. All he needed to see at the moment was anybody coming and going through the alley. Since there was no space between the houses, there were only two ways in or out back there, and Haley could see the other end of the alley from his position.

He got his phone out and pretended to do stuff on it to try to give himself an inconspicuous appearance. The last thing he needed was somebody seeing a stranger hanging around and calling the cops on him. Not that plunging his face into his phone was much of a cover, but it was all he had at the moment. With his back to a concrete wall, Haley slid down and sat on the ground, still keeping an eye out.

As it turned out, Haley didn't have any better luck in the alley than he did waiting out front. He sat there for several hours, remaining there glued to the ground well past the time it got dark out. The kids playing basketball went inside a long time ago, leaving Haley back there by himself. Just him and his thoughts. And his thoughts right now were telling him this was a mistake. It just didn't seem normal.

With the battery on his phone getting low, Haley didn't want to stay back there too much longer, just in case he needed to call for help for some reason. Assuming that nothing else was going to happen, Haley figured since it was past ten o'clock, that he was going to call it a night. He walked back around to the front, getting in his car. He plugged his phone in to charge, calling Jones at the same time.

"Hey, there's just nothing happening here," Haley said, a high level of frustration clearly evident in his voice.

"Still nothing, huh?"

Jones had a slight sound of frustration in his voice as well. Even when he did, he usually tried to hide it, wanting to seem as level-headed as possible. He always felt that when Recker or Haley were frustrated with something, it was his job to calm them down and make sure they continued to think reasonably and clearly. Frustration led to impatience, which led to mistakes, which could lead to injury or death. Jones made sure that didn't happen, even if he was frustrated himself.

"This is a waste of time," Haley continued. "I mean, there's just nothing. What about this girl? She just ditch work and turn invisible with these guys?"

Jones put two fingers over his mouth and his thumb under his chin as he looked at several of his computer screens, examining, and reexamining every piece of information he had at his disposal. Haley was right that it seemed odd that he saw no signs of activity, but everything Jones had was telling him the gang was inside that building.

"I think I gotta get a closer look," Haley said.

"No," Jones replied, not willing to chance such a move yet. "We're not there yet."

In truth, Jones may have sanctioned that move if the gang they were looking for only had two or three members, but with at least six that they knew of, and possibly more, the odds were simply too great. Especially at the moment, when they didn't need to rush into a bad situation. They could afford to let it play out.

"Let's give it another day and see what transpires," Jones said.

Haley reluctantly agreed and remained in front of the house for another hour or so, wanting to give it a final look before he called it a night. Nothing had changed though. He left for home, ready to get a good night's sleep. Once he got home, he called Mia to check on Recker's condition.

"How's he doing?" Haley asked.

"Good," Mia answered. "He'll probably be ready to go back to work in another day or two."

"Glad to hear it."

"Wish I was."

Haley could tell by the tone of her voice that she wasn't very enthusiastic about Recker returning to the job. He didn't need Mia to expand further, but he knew that she probably would have preferred Recker to leave for good.

"Everything going OK?" Mia asked. "Hope Mike not

being there hasn't put too much stress on you or anything."

"No, everything's fine. Just been on some boring stakeout for the past two days. Nothing happening at all."

"You sound tired."

"Yeah, I'm gonna get some sleep soon. If you need anything, let me know."

"I will. Thank you for being a good friend. And for showing up when you did the other night."

"You guys are like family to me now. No thanks are necessary."

Haley did get a good amount of sleep. The most he'd gotten in the past week. Before leaving his apartment to get to the office, he called Jones to see what the plans were for today. He cringed a little when Jones told him to just bypass the office and start stakeout duties on the Mendoza house immediately. Haley just knew it was going to be another one of those long and boring days. Nevertheless, Haley did as he was instructed and parked in front of the house, though he figured he'd change things up by parking on the other side of the street, hoping it would change his luck.

Unfortunately, the day would go by the same as the others. Not one sign of activity in or around the house. Haley spent ten hours sitting in the car, keeping his eyes peeled. He was convinced that nothing was going to happen, and he couldn't shake the feeling that nobody was even inside. He called Jones once again to convey his feelings on the matter.

"David, I'm all for patience and not rushing into things, but this is getting a little ridiculous."

"I understand your frustrations," Jones replied.

"Maybe Kirby and the others I can understand keeping a low profile, but the girl isn't wanted for anything. There's no need for her to hunker down in there and not come out for anything. If anything, they would use her for a runner."

Jones himself let out a sigh. "I would tend to agree."

"It's getting dark now. I'm thinking it's time for a look-see."

Jones rubbed his forehead as he thought about the suggestion, still not thrilled with the idea of letting Haley go in closer without backup. Haley tried to entice him as much as he could.

"I promise I won't engage or anything."

"Well, just how would you go about that?" Jones asked.

"I dunno. I'll knock on the door and see if anyone answers."

"You'll do what now?"

"Obviously, I won't be empty handed or anything," Haley replied. "I'll just walk up there with a pizza and see what happens."

"You're gonna go get a pizza… and then what? Pretend you have the wrong address or something?"

"You got it."

Jones scratched his head and closed his eyes, thinking that was one of the worst ideas he's heard.

"You're going to go buy a pizza?"

"No," Haley answered. "I got one in the back."

"You have a pizza in the car?"

"Well not a full pizza. Just the box."

"Why are you travelling around with just a pizza box?"

"Well, it's kinda like this... last week I ordered a pizza at home."

"OK?"

"And I got to thinking that maybe it might come in handy someday. Kind of like Mike does with his police badge. Just something to get things going."

"You mean you've actually been giving this a lot of thought previous to this conversation?"

"Oh yeah," Haley replied.

"I really don't even know what to say."

"I've actually been eager to try this out and see how it works."

"And you don't think they'll be alarmed to see you standing outside their door with a pizza?"

"Lots of pizzas are delivered at this time of night. No biggie."

Jones put his hand on his forehead, resigned to let this play out, even though it was against his better judgment. "God help me for letting you go through with this."

"Relax, it'll work. I'm gonna get everything ready. I'll let you know how it goes."

Jones sat at his desk and said a prayer, hoping this wouldn't end in disaster. Haley got out of his car to open the trunk to get the pizza box. He double checked his weapon, then put it in his belt, pulling his shirt down over top of it. Pretending like there was an actual hot pizza in there, he carried it like he'd been delivering pizza's all his life. He went up the concrete steps to the Mendoza row home and opened the screen door. He knocked on the door, listening for any signs of people inside. He still didn't hear anything though. No low voices trying to be quiet, no scurrying feet trying to see who it was, no nothing. It only served to raise Haley's suspicions even further.

Haley knocked on the door again, even louder this time. "Hello! Pizza!"

He still didn't get a reply. Haley's patience had just about run out now. He took a look around to make sure no neighbors or people walking along the street were staring at him. He put the pizza box on the ground, took out a credit card, and started to work on the lock. Luckily, there wasn't a deadbolt on the door, not that Haley couldn't have still gotten it open, it just would have taken a little more time.

As Haley slowly pushed the door open, he removed his gun, not sure if he was walking into a hornet's nest or not. It was pitch dark, but Haley didn't want to go for a light yet. He gradually walked through the living room, which led to the dining area and the kitchen. There was no one in sight. Seeing the door for the basement, Haley opened it and flicked on the light. Someone might have known he was coming, but he wasn't walking down there blind.

There wasn't much to the basement as it wasn't finished. It was basically just one big storage area, but there were only a few boxes. Haley went back upstairs and turned on the kitchen light, just so he could see a little better. He wasn't really concerned with anyone else at that point. He went up the stairs, not seeing or hearing a sign of life within the house. It was almost eerie.

Haley cleared three bedrooms and a bathroom, none of which had any bodies in it, either living or dead. He went back down to the living room and checked the window to make sure nobody was coming. It was a ghost town in there. He then called Jones to let him know he was alive and well along with the fact that he was inside the residence.

"Just wanted to let you know that I'm not dead."

"Always a reassuring thing," Jones said.

"Yeah, anyway, I'm inside the house."

"And?"

"And there's no one here."

"What? Are you sure?"

"Uh, yeah, pretty sure. I just cleared every room, top to bottom. There's nothing here."

As they talked, Haley turned on a couple more lights and started looking around. He still wasn't sure if someone was living there or not, so he tried to move quickly.

"How bizarre," Jones said.

"That ain't the half of it," Haley replied, going into the kitchen area after coming up empty in the living room. "I'm not finding anything so far that anybody is even living here."

Haley opened up the refrigerator, the freezer, as well as a couple of cabinets. Unless someone was there and living on dust and tap water, it just wasn't happening. Everything was empty.

"Uh, David, there is nothing in this kitchen. The fridge is empty, not even a moldy old piece of cheese."

Jones looked at his computer screens, wondering how he could have gotten everything so wrong. The two men were silent for a minute as Haley went upstairs to check the rooms. There was nothing of value anywhere, except one thing that caught Haley's eye on a table near a bed. It was a phone.

"I got something," Haley said, picking the phone up.

"What is it?"

"A phone." Haley started scrolling through it, but there were no names or contacts in it. He checked the call history, and it was blank.

"Anything?"

"No. It's clean."

A concerned look came over Jones' face, worried about what it all meant. Everything that led him to that house was sound, every piece of information was correct. Nobody being there was worrisome. A phone being left behind even more so. Then it came to him. He stared at the screen that had Bradshaw's phone number on it.

"Chris, do me a favor and call me from that phone that you just found."

"What?" Haley asked, thinking it a strange request.

"Just call me from that phone. If what happens is what I think will happen, I may have some answers on this mystery."

"OK."

Haley did as his boss asked and called Jones from the abandoned phone. Once Jones' phone started to ring, he immediately looked at the screen in front of him, seeing a red dot blinking. It was the same phone that he was tracking Bradshaw with.

"It's her phone," Jones said.

"What sense does that make? I mean, why leave the phone here?" Haley let out a very audible sigh. "I just don't get it. If this is her phone, why isn't she here? Or anyone else for that matter. Where'd they go?"

"I believe the answer to that is they weren't there to begin with."

"Say what?"

"If I have to make an educated guess right now, I'd say this is all a setup."

"What? Why? Who?"

"First things first, you need to get out of there as quickly as possible," Jones said, his voice crackling as he was afraid of what might be lurking nearby.

Hearing the urgency in his voice, Haley hurried down the steps and toward the front door. Just before he got there though, Bradshaw's phone rang, indicating a text message. Haley got a bad feeling about this and was almost hesitant to check, fearing what it might say. Even feeling the bad vibes, Haley let Jones know something came through, and then read it.

"*Silencer!*" the message read. "*Took you long enough to get here. I've been waiting.*"

"*Who are you?*" Haley replied.

"*Not important. What is important is that I now know how you get information. Consider that avenue closed.*"

"*What are you talking about?*"

Haley waited a couple of minutes but there was no reply. He then got back on the phone with Jones to see what the next move was.

"I'll just come back to the office," Haley said.

As Haley walked out the front door, Jones started thinking about the messages just sent to Haley.

"Chris, don't go outside!" Jones warned.

"I'm already outside."

"Go back in. Hurry!"

"What? Why?"

"Just do it."

Haley turned around just as a shot rang out. Haley moved just in the nick of time, though he still got hit. Luckily, it was a glancing blow off his arm in what basically amounted to a scratch. Haley got inside and locked the door, scurrying over to a window and looking out to see where the shot came from.

"What the hell is going on here?"

"This was all a setup," Jones answered. "This was planned."

"What are you talking about?"

"Don't worry about that now. Right now, just worry about getting out of there."

"I'll duck out the back way."

"Be careful. I have a feeling your night may not be done."

# 9

Haley flew down the steps to the basement, rushing toward the back door. He wasn't sure what was going on or who was after him, but those were questions for another time. Right now, he just had to worry about escaping in one piece. He figured if someone was waiting for him out front, there was a good chance someone was waiting in back too. He had to be cautious, but there weren't a lot of places to hide in the alleyway. That was both good and bad. Bad that he couldn't really take cover behind anything, but good that the other guy couldn't either.

What made things worse was Haley had no idea how many people he was up against. Could've been one. Might've been fifty. Still, one shot had already been fired and heard, so the police might have been on the way, though he didn't hear any sirens yet. But that still meant he couldn't stay very long. He had to go, regardless of what was out there.

Haley threw open the door quickly and violently, hoping to get a reaction and a quick trigger from whoever was out there, that way he could hear the direction the shots were coming from. He wasn't disappointed. A bullet ripped through the door, leaving a hole through the center of it. It was only one shot, leaving Haley to believe only one man was out there, and it came from his left.

Haley could've just run out the door fast, jumped and rolled on the ground, giving his shooter a tough target to aim at, but it also would've been tough for Haley to find the man, while leaving himself wide open. Instead, he got down on the ground and crawled. Most people don't look down when looking for someone, they usually look straight ahead, and that's what Haley was counting on.

Haley poked his head out the door and quickly tried to find his target. With not getting his head blown off yet, he figured his assessment of the situation was correct so far. After squinting for a few seconds and trying to look through the darkness, Haley finally found his man. He saw a pair of legs standing by some trash cans not too far away.

Wanting to take extra precaution and not assume anything, Haley took an extra couple of minutes to look to his right also, making sure nobody was over there either. He didn't see anyone though. Haley wasn't taking any chances yet and wasn't about to make himself a target either. Still lying on the ground, he brought his gun around in front of him, and took aim at the man. Haley pulled the trigger, the bullet going through the man's leg, shattering his shin.

The man dropped to the ground in agony. The gun flew out of his hand as his hands instinctively went to his throbbing leg, holding his shin as he cried out in pain. As the man writhed around on the ground, Haley took aim again. He probably could have just fled the scene and left the man alive, but he didn't want to take the chance of him taking a pot shot at him on the run. Besides, the man had tried to kill him, so now all bets were off. As the man lifted his back off the ground to look down at his leg, Haley fired once more. A direct hit that went into the lower part of the man's chest, killing him immediately.

Haley got to his knees as he continued to look around, making sure he didn't run into a bullet himself. Satisfied that no one else was around, he stood up fully and started walking out of the alley. He stayed close to the wall though and continually kept checking all around. When he finally got to the end of the alley without incident, he breathed a sigh of relief. There was still the shooter from the front, but Haley figured he was long gone.

As he walked along the sidewalk to get around to the front of the buildings, a huge explosion was heard. It rattled the area and Haley lost his balance a little, though he still remained on his feet. The explosion came from the area of the house, so Haley started running in that direction to see what had transpired. He quickly stopped once he turned the corner and saw what it was. His car was on fire and looked like it had just been driven through a war zone, charred, glass blown out, pieces of metal bent and twisted, a couple doors that were thrown across the street, not to mention the fire that was shooting up through where the windows used to be.

Haley wasn't even mad. He was just stunned. He was too shocked to be angry. He just stood there for a minute, frozen as he looked at what used to be his vehicle. Then he heard police and fire sirens, with several patrol cars zooming down the street to begin blocking things off. Knowing there was nothing else he could do there, and since his car was torn to shreds, Haley just backed away and started walking. He called Jones to let him know he was on foot.

"Hey, just wanted to let you know that I'm good."

"Thankfully," Jones said. "I was worried. What about the shooter?"

"Well, there were two that I know of. There was another one waiting in back for me."

"Oh?"

"Yeah, he's dead. The one in front got away."

"Get a look at either of them?"

"No, I probably should have checked out the guy I killed, but I was just too interested in getting out of there. Wasn't sure how many there might have been."

"No, you did the right thing," Jones replied. "I can probably find out later, anyway. Are you on your way back here?"

"Well, you see, that's kind of a problem."

"What? Why?"

"Well... my car blew up."

"Excuse me?"

"Yeah, my car is literally on fire right now. Police and fire are here putting it out."

"Uh...," Jones murmured, not even sure what to say.

"My thoughts exactly."

"What happened?"

"Beats me. Came out of the alley and started walking back to the front, then I heard an explosion. Came around the corner and saw my car on fire."

"They knew it was you. They knew you were there the whole time."

"I guess so," Haley said. "This whole thing's pretty strange."

"Not so strange once you hear what I think is going on."

"What's that?"

"I'll tell you about it later."

"It'll have to be much later since I'm walking."

"Where are you? I'll come get you."

Haley told him to come to a nearby convenience store, where Haley would stop in for a soda while he waited. About half an hour later, Jones arrived. Once Haley got in the car and they started back for the office, he was eager for Jones to start explaining his theory.

"So, what's going on here?" Haley asked.

"We got played. This whole thing, starting from the jump was planned as a setup."

"I don't follow."

"Tyrell called Mike about something going down in the jewelry store, right?"

"Yeah."

"I believe that was planned specifically to get him down there so they could kill him."

"Why?" Haley asked.

"More on that in a minute. With it failing, they went to Plan B, which was the Mendoza house. They knew we'd be tracking the group and come across Bradshaw. Knowing I'd probably be able to trace the phone, they left it in the house, so we'd specifically go there."

"So, while I was watching the house, they were watching me, waiting for me to go inside."

"Precisely."

"That still leaves a question of who," Haley said. "This Kirby group isn't sophisticated enough to pull something like this off on their own. We've never even tangled with them before, there'd be no reason for them to do this."

"You're right about that. They're not behind it. I believe they've been used for pawns in this scheme."

"Pawns? Who would want to knock us off? Who would even have a reason? And who's dirty enough to do it?"

Jones gave him a menacing kind of look, persuading him to think harder. Haley thought for a second, one name popping up in his head in particular.

"Vincent? We're not on bad terms with him though. And he knows Tyrell."

"Close. Nowak."

"Nowak? Why? I mean, we've tangled with her before, but we haven't interacted with her lately."

"Remember, she wants to take over the city. She can't do that unless she gets rid of Vincent and us. Vincent's her competition and we'd be like a cloud hanging over her head. Also, when Tyrell told Mike about the plan, he said something about Nowak, though he wasn't sure she was involved."

"So back at the house, did they think they were shooting at Mike, or me?"

"I'm not sure. It doesn't really matter though, does it?"

"Wait a minute, wait a minute," Haley said, thinking about the strange text messages he received.

"What is it?"

"The message said something about knowing how we get information and that the avenue would be closed. There's a meaning in there, a warning."

Jones looked at Haley in horror, knowing what it meant. "Tyrell."

Haley returned the horrific look. "They wanted to see who on the street is working with us."

"And now they know. They found their man."

"We gotta warn him."

Haley immediately got out his phone and dialed Tyrell's number to warn him of what they feared to be an impending attack on his life. It kept ringing, but eventually went to voicemail.

"He's not picking up," Haley said in a panic.

"Keep trying."

Haley tried several more times, all with the same result. It was unusual for Tyrell not to answer for this long. His phone was usually close by. Jones and Haley began fearing that the worst had happened.

"Let's just drive to his house and see if he's there," Haley said, praying that they wouldn't be too late.

**10**

———

Haley tried several more times to call Tyrell on the way to his house, still to no avail. When they finally arrived at his house, they ran toward the front door. It was late at night, a little after eleven, and hoped they wouldn't scare his mother or brother, but they figured it had to be done under the circumstances. Haley pounded on the door, not sure if anyone was sleeping or not, but needed to get someone's attention. A few minutes later, they saw the curtain from the window move and someone looking out. Then the door opened. It was Darnell.

"Mr. Haley, Mr. Jones, what's wrong?"

"Darnell, where's your brother?" Haley asked.

"Uh, I don't know. He got a message about an hour ago and left. Said he'd be back soon."

"A message? From who?"

"He said it was from Mr. Recker."

Jones and Haley looked at each other, knowing Recker

sent no such message. Still, just to be sure, Haley immediately called Mia.

"Chris? Everything OK?"

"I'm not sure yet. Is Mike there?"

"Of course he is. Why?"

"Did he go somewhere?" Haley asked. "Or is he planning on going somewhere?"

"Of course not. He's been here all night. What's going on?"

"It's a long story. And it's been a long night. I got shot at, my car blown up, and Tyrell told his brother that he got a message from Mike to meet him somewhere about an hour ago."

"Oh my, are you OK?"

"Yeah, I'm fine. Just trying to figure out what's going on."

"Well, Mike's been sleeping for the last three hours," Mia said. "And his phone isn't near him."

"That's what I was afraid of."

"What's going on?"

"Someone's trying to take all of us, and everyone associated with us, out of the game."

Mia had a lot more questions but didn't want to keep Haley tied up knowing Tyrell's safety was at stake. "I'll let you go so you can concentrate on finding Tyrell."

"OK, thanks."

"Let me know when you find him."

"I will."

Haley looked at Jones and shook his head. Seeing the

concerned look on their faces, Darnell was starting to get worried himself.

"What's going on? Why you looking for my brother?"

"Did he mention where he was going?" Jones asked.

Darnell shook his head. "No, just said he was meeting him and would be back soon. That's all he said." Seeing the disappointed looks they were giving each other, Darnell knew something was wrong. "What is it?"

"Mike's at home," Haley said. "He's got a concussion and hasn't left his place in a few days. He didn't send Tyrell any message."

Darnell looked confused. "I don't understand. Why would Tyrell say it was from him if it wasn't?"

"How did they contact him?" Jones asked. "By phone?"

"Yeah."

"We think somebody..."

Jones was interrupted by Haley grabbing his arm. He didn't think it was a good idea to tell Darnell the truth and have him worry all night about their suspicions.

"We don't know what's going on," Haley said. "That's why we're looking for him. You don't have any idea where he might have gone?"

"Nah. He really don't talk to me much about his business. He tries to keep me away from all that."

"OK. Well, if he comes back, or you hear from him, tell him to call us as soon as possible, all right?"

"Yeah, I will."

Jones and Haley dejectedly walked back to their car, unsure what to do next. They had no way of knowing where Tyrell might have gone.

"You sure we shouldn't have told him what's going on?" Jones asked.

"He doesn't need to know. He's just a kid. He shouldn't have something like that on his mind the entire night. Besides, we don't even know for sure Tyrell's life is in danger. We could be wrong."

"I don't think we are."

"Maybe not. But if we're right, Darnell will know soon enough, anyway."

Jones sighed. "Well, I guess the only thing we can do right now is go back to the office and I can tap into his phone."

"That's gonna take time we don't have."

"I know, but what else can we do?"

They drove back to the office, prepared to have a very long night. Once there, Jones immediately hopped on a computer and started typing away. It wasn't long before Jones had found what he was looking for.

"His last call was exactly one hour and forty-two minutes ago," Jones said.

"Who from?" Haley asked.

"It's an unlisted number."

"Figures. What about texts?"

"Nothing in the last three hours," Jones replied. "And the last one he had was to his brother letting him know he was on his way home."

"So, we're not any closer to finding him."

"Unfortunately, no."

The two of them sat back in their chairs, knowing there was nothing else they could do. Nothing but wait and hope that their fears were unfounded and go by without incident. After several hours of not hearing anything, and Jones was continually checking both police and hospital records, the wait was starting to get to them.

"Feels like a wake in here," Haley said.

"I know."

"I don't ever remember feeling so helpless before. Here we are waiting for word of something terrible happening and there's nothing we can do about it."

"Well, I guess we can take solace in that no news is good news," Jones said.

"Who says? No news is even worse. That means he still hasn't turned up yet, cause if he had, he would've called us by now."

"True."

As the night wore on, the feeling in their stomachs that a catastrophe was just around the corner only increased. Once three o'clock came, they were about to call it a night.

"I think we might as well get a few hours of sleep at this point," Jones said. "There's really not much else we can do here."

"Yeah, I guess you're right. Just sitting and waiting for the bottom to drop out isn't doing us much good."

They stood up and pushed their chairs in, Haley stretching his arms out. Before they were able to pack up for the night, one of Jones' computers started beeping.

"What's that?" Haley asked.

"An alert."

"You've got an alert for just about everything at this point, don't you?"

"It does make things easier," Jones answered, sitting back down to investigate.

"What's this one?"

"Oh, no."

"What? What's wrong?"

"It's Tyrell."

"He's dead?"

Jones looked up and sighed, more of relief than anything. "No, thank heavens. But it looks as though he was badly injured."

"What happened?" Haley asked, sitting back down as well.

"He was shot. Multiple times."

"Bad? How do you know?"

"I put his name into every hospital in the city and a thirty-mile radius outside of it so I'd get an alert if his name popped into the system."

"How bad?"

"Looks as though he's in the emergency room undergoing surgery," Jones replied.

"What's his prognosis?"

"Too soon to tell. All we can do now is pray."

"Should we let Mike know?"

"Yes, but let's wait until the morning."

"We're already in the morning," Haley said.

"I mean, much later. After we've all had a chance to get a little sleep. The only thing we could do now by telling him is make him worry."

"Something tells me he'll find out before we say a word about it."

"Yes, I think that's probably likely. And something else tells me that we shall be seeing our friend sooner rather than later."

"Is that good or bad?" Haley asked.

"I don't know. I guess we'll see when it happens."

**11**

———

Recker woke up about ten o'clock, smelling bacon and eggs cooking on the stove. He sat up on the edge of the bed, actually feeling good for a change. There was no headache, or tiredness, or ringing in his head, all his symptoms seemed to be gone. He walked into the kitchen, instantly getting greeted with a hug and a kiss from Mia as soon as she saw him.

"How are you feeling?"

"Good," Recker said.

"No, really? Don't lie to me."

Recker laughed. "No, I'm telling you the truth. I really feel good. I'm fine."

"You're not just saying that so you can get out of here?"

Recker gave her another kiss on the lips. "Why would I wanna do that? Staying here all alone with you isn't a punishment."

"Well, I would hope not. But I know how you are. You don't like being cooped up in one place for too long."

"I guess you're right about that, but not in this instance. I couldn't think of a better spot or person to be cooped up with than you."

They began passionately kissing, which probably would've led to some other things, but Recker's phone started ringing, which Mia had put down on the kitchen counter. They stopped kissing, and Mia hung her head, putting it on Recker's chest, disappointed that they were interrupted.

"And so, it begins," Mia said.

"I don't have to answer it."

"No, answer, I doubt they'd be calling you if it wasn't important."

Recker smiled at her and gave her another kiss before walking over to his phone. He picked it up, expecting to see Jones or Haley's name on the screen. He was a little perplexed to see Darnell calling. He knew something had to be up.

"Darnell? What's going on? Everything OK?"

"Mr. Recker, I'm so glad to finally get through. I tried calling you a few times already. I wasn't sure what was going on."

Recker could tell by the sound of his voice that something bad had happened. Darnell had a slight tremble to his voice. "What's the matter?"

"It's my brother. Tyrell."

A sick feeling immediately came over Recker, afraid of what he was about to hear. "What about him?"

"You don't know yet?"

"No. What is it?"

"He's been shot," Darnell said. "He's in the hospital."

"Is he gonna be OK?"

"He's in recovery right now, but the doctor just talked to me and my mom, and they think he's gonna make it."

Recker let out a huge sigh of relief. "That's good. What happened?"

"I don't know. Tyrell isn't really talking much right now. They want him to conserve his energy. All I know is last night he told me he got a message from you and he was going out. Then Mr. Jones and Mr. Haley came over a little later asking where Tyrell was. Then in the middle of the night we got a call from the police saying Tyrell was shot and was at the hospital."

"Is he allowed visitors right now?"

"No, not right now, not for a little bit."

"OK, well, as soon as he is, you let me know and I'll be over, OK?"

"I will. Who would wanna do that to him?"

"I don't know. But I promise you I will find out."

As soon as he hung up, Mia knew it was about Tyrell. Remembering the call she got the night before from Haley, it would be the only reason Darnell was calling. She too was worried about him, though she didn't want to tell Recker about it before she thought he was well enough to handle the news. Now it appeared she didn't have to worry about it since Recker seemed back to normal.

"Is Tyrell OK?"

"He was shot last night," Recker answered. "He's in the hospital but the doctors think he'll be OK."

"Thank goodness. What happened?"

"They don't know yet. Something about getting a message from me."

"Yeah, Chris called last night saying something about that. He didn't go into details though. Just that they were looking for him."

"I gotta figure out what's going on here."

"Oh yeah," Mia said, remembering more of the details of her conversation with Haley. "And Chris said he got shot at and his car blown up."

"What?"

"I don't know. That's what he said."

"I go away for a few days and it feels like World War Three started."

A disappointed look came over Mia's face. "I guess that means you're going back to work today."

Recker took her in his arms. "I have to. My friends are getting shot at and blown up. I can't sit on the sidelines and let it all happen."

"Just make sure you're careful please."

"Aren't I always?" he said with a smile.

Mia looked at him like she couldn't believe he even asked. "Just try to be more careful."

"I promise."

They sat down and finished eating breakfast. Once they were done, Recker gave Mia a kiss and left for the office. He thought about calling Jones first to see what was going on and to let him know he was on the way, but then thought he'd rather surprise him by just showing up without any warning.

Jones and Haley were already at the office, both typing away on their respective computers. They seemed to have a lot on their plate. They were keeping an eye on Tyrell's condition, trying to track down Kirby and his crew, and trying to get a connection to Nowak in all of this. When they heard the door open, they quickly jumped, not knowing who it was, and not figuring on Recker suddenly appearing.

"Hey, look what the wind blew in," Haley said with a smile, walking over to Recker as he walked in the door to shake hands and welcome him back.

"Yeah, just never know what's gonna crawl in here."

"Michael, I take it you're fully recovered," Jones said.

"Good as new. Feel fine."

"I hope you got a clean bill of health from Mia. She does know you are here, doesn't she?"

"Yes, David, my doctor cleared me to resume all activities. I'm good to go."

"Good."

"So, who wants to tell me about what's going on?" Recker asked.

"Going on?"

"Yeah, you know, about Tyrell being shot, Chris' car being blown up, being shot at, you know, that."

"Oh, you know all about that already, huh?"

"Mia doesn't miss much."

"Indeed, she doesn't," Jones said. "Well, pull up a chair and we'll go over everything in detail."

Recker and Haley went over to the couch and sat down as Jones sat behind the desk. Jones and Haley then alternated telling different parts of the story, remembering every detail exactly and not leaving the slightest bit of information out. After they were finished, Recker was silent for a minute, staring at the wall and letting everything soak in.

"Nowak orchestrated this whole thing, huh?" Recker asked.

"How big a long shot was this though?" Haley said. "I mean, what made her think we'd be at that jewelry store? And then everything after that?"

"You're assuming this was the only card she's been playing. What if she's been putting stuff like this out for weeks or months? Trying to find out who's leaking the information, where we're getting information from, everything about the operation. She might have reenacted that exact scene for weeks with different people, waiting to see who bites. Then when we finally show up, she'll know where and who that information came from."

"Makes sense. That's a lot of effort though, isn't it? Especially when she's cranking up the war on Vincent. I mean, why take us both on at the same time?"

"Maybe she assumed she'd be taking us both on at the same time anyway," Jones said. "Considering our history with Vincent, that's not an unreasonable assumption to make."

"Plus, if it worked, she wouldn't have had to worry about it," Recker replied. "She almost got both of us. Me in the alley, Chris in that house."

"And she didn't even get Tyrell either," Haley said. "A lot of almosts, but not quites. If her plan was to take us out before getting to Vincent, she failed miserably."

"Well, we'll just have to make sure she pays, won't we?"

Jones looked at Recker, knowing he had vengeance in mind. Not that any of them could be blamed for it, but Jones hated the fact that they were getting drawn into another conflict with a criminal element. In his mind, it just took attention and focus off of people that could have really used their help. That's what bothered him the most. The people who might slip through the cracks because their concentration was diverted elsewhere.

For the next couple of hours, the three of them began discussing different options that were on the table. After going through various scenarios, they finally settled on something they all could agree on. They wouldn't rush into anything, instead, making sure that they moved as quickly and as quietly as possible so as not to alert Nowak they were coming for her, even if she now suspected they would be, anyway. They didn't want to engage in some long war, taking months or years to get to her. They wanted to get into a position where the first chance they had at her, they would succeed at taking her down. In order to do that, they'd have to move quietly, almost make it seem like they weren't coming at all. And when she least suspected it, then they would pounce. Just before they were about to leave the office, Haley got an idea that would be beneficial to all parties.

"I just thought of something," Haley said.

"Yeah?" Recker replied.

"Why don't we just tell Vincent that we've changed our mind and will help him in getting rid of Nowak?"

"Why?"

"So he thinks we're doing it to help him and will owe us one down the road. He won't know we're doing it as much for ourselves as for him."

Recker thought about it for a minute, looking over to Jones to see what he thought. By the look on Jones' face, he could tell he wasn't enamored with the idea.

"I don't know if I want to get into bed with Vincent over this," Jones said. "Even if it is beneficial to do so, at some point we should probably break free of him, or else we will always be exchanging favors."

"The question is whether that time is now?" Recker asked.

"Honestly, he's probably got more info and dirt on her than we do right now," Haley said.

"Perhaps," Jones said. "But that is only temporary. Give me enough time and I'm sure I will have mountains of information above what he does."

"I say we do it," Recker said, looking Jones in the eyes. "I don't like anyone gunning for us. As far as I'm concerned, right now, it's all hands on deck. The more people we have against Nowak, the better off we are. Everything else takes a back seat to that. Or else, who knows what happens next time? Maybe she actually succeeds in knocking one of us off."

Jones nodded, understanding his point.

"And let's not forget that she's gonna get word at some

point, if she hasn't already, that Tyrell isn't dead," Haley said. "She might try for him again."

"Well then, let's make sure that doesn't happen," Jones replied.

"Agreed," Recker said. "Let's pay Vincent a visit."

Recker got out his phone and was about to call Vincent when his phone started ringing first. It was Darnell again.

"I just wanted to let you know that Tyrell is now stable. He's talking and can have visitors now."

"That's great news," Recker replied. "I'll leave right now to come down."

"Good. He was asking about you. I'll tell him you're on the way."

"Thanks for letting me know."

After Recker hung up, he relayed the news to the others. All of them wanted to go see him.

"Should one of us stay here and start working on things?" Jones asked.

Recker shook his head. "No, an hour or two isn't gonna set us back much. After all he's done for us, I think he deserves all of us to be there."

"I would agree."

"We'll visit Tyrell first. Then we'll start working on payback."

## 12

Once Recker, Jones, and Haley arrived at the hospital and were directed to Tyrell's room, they quickly went to his room, eager to see how he was doing. When they went in, Tyrell was just lying there with his eyes closed. No one else was there. Tyrell heard his visitors come in though and opened his eyes and turned his head to look at them. Recker, Jones, and Haley each approached the bed and shook Tyrell's hand, who was genuinely glad to see the trio.

"Where's your mom and Darnell?" Recker asked as he sat down on a chair next to the bed.

"Oh, they only allow a couple people in here at a time so when I told them you were coming, they went down to the cafeteria for some food."

Jones and Haley also took a seat, towards the end of the bed.

"What have they told you about your prognosis?" Jones asked.

Tyrell smiled. "It's good to see you, Prof. I wasn't sure you were gonna come down here for little old me."

"Please. You're like family to all of us. Nothing would keep any of us away."

"Good to hear. Anyway, they say I'll be alright. Probably be in here for another week or two, depending on how I feel, I guess. I dunno, they keep saying stuff, and it kinda goes in one ear and out the other. Too much doctor speak, you know?"

"So, what happened?" Recker asked.

"I got shot."

"I know that. But why? Why did you go? You know I never send a message to you through a third party. Why would you fall for that?"

"I didn't," Tyrell answered. "I knew it wasn't you."

"Then why'd you go?"

"I wanted to see what was going on. I figured if someone was calling me, telling me you sent them, then that meant somebody knew we were working together. I wanted to see who it was and how they knew it."

"Why didn't you just wait for us to check it out?"

"I dunno. I figured I could handle it on my own."

"Too risky, man."

Tyrell laughed, though it hurt to do so, and he covered his ribs with his arms. "Now you're telling me. Yeah, if I had to do it over again, I probably wouldn't go. But at the time I thought I could handle it."

"I'm sorry," Recker said. "It's my fault."

"Hey, you didn't tell me to go. That was my own doing."

"Yeah, but if you didn't know me, then you wouldn't be here."

"Hey, don't start up with that," Tyrell said. "I knew exactly what I was doing and what I was getting into when I hooked up with you guys all them years ago. You ain't gotta treat me with kid gloves, man, I know the risks. I've been taking them long before I ever knew you. It's just part of the deal, we all know that."

"Yeah, I know."

"If you really feel bad and wanna help me, then you'll find out who did this and make sure they never get a second chance."

"You know I will," Recker replied. "What can you tell us about what happened?"

"Got a call from someone, said no caller ID on the phone, told me you were busy and wanted to meet down at Rittenhouse."

"Did they say my name specifically?"

"Yeah, they said Recker wanted me to come down for a meet."

"Man or woman?"

"It was a guy," Tyrell answered.

"Recognize the voice?"

"Nah, never heard it before."

"Any idea who shot you? Description? Anything?"

Tyrell shook his head. "Never saw the dude. Shots came from behind. Never saw what hit me. Could've been one guy or twenty for all I know."

"I'm gonna need the name of the guy who told you about that jewelry store thing you told me about."

"What? Why?" Tyrell asked, never letting the name of one of his informants slip out before.

"I think he set us both up."

"What? You're crazy, man. What are you talking about?"

"Just think about it," Recker said. "Whoever slipped that information to you, was looking to see if you knew me. I went there, I got shot. We tracked the group to a place in the northeast where Chris got shot at and his car blown up."

"What?" Tyrell asked, looking at Haley, the first he was hearing about it. "You got your car blown up?"

"Yeah, long story," Haley said. "Happened only a few hours before your incident."

"See? Fits the pattern," Recker said. "They wanted to see who the guy on the ground was who was working with us. Once I rolled on that call, they knew it was you. They tried to take me out, tried to take Chris out, then tried to take you out."

As Recker continued explaining his theory, Tyrell was intently listening, thinking it all made sense. By the time Recker was done, Tyrell was convinced he was right. They all got set up.

"Jerome," Tyrell said. "That no good mother..."

"Jerome? That's the guy?"

"Yeah. Thought I could trust him."

"Apparently not," Recker said.

"Yeah, just wait for me to get out of here and kick that dude's ass myself."

"Well, as much as I'd like to give you that opportunity, we'd kind of like to talk to him before you get out of here."

"Saving all the fun for yourself?"

"If it makes you feel any better, I promise we won't kill him."

"Yeah," Tyrell said, his face lighting up at the prospect of working the guy over. "Yeah, leave a piece of him for me. I got some words, along with some other things, that I wanna say and do to him."

"You know where we can find him?"

"That weasel might have buried himself into the ground now for all I know."

"Well, we're gonna need to talk to him."

"I can send him a message letting him know I'm alive and well and wanna talk about something."

"You think he'd respond to that?" Recker asked.

"Oh yeah. He ain't gonna think that I'm on to him or nothing. Just let me know when you're ready, time and place, and I'll send him a message."

"OK. It'll probably be sometime tonight. I wanna move quickly on this."

"Sounds good. I can text him before you guys leave here. You know who's behind all this?"

"We think it's Nowak. She either thinks we're with Vincent or she just wants to take us out independently of him. Either way, it's clear she thinks we're a threat to her."

"What about that jewelry store?" Tyrell asked.

"I think she just hired a crew and told them what to do. We're on their trail too, but there's nothing in their background that suggests they're capable of pulling something like this off. Plus, we've never had a run-in with them before, so there's no reason they'd be targeting us or you."

"Damn Nowak."

"They tell you what you gotta do when you leave here?" Haley asked. "Rehab or anything?"

"I dunno, man, they said some stuff, but like I said, I wasn't really paying attention to all that. They talked to my mom about everything, so she knows what's going on. I'm sure I gotta take some time off to heal up and everything. However long that'll take."

"Well, you just make sure you don't rush back and hurt yourself even more," Recker said, tapping Tyrell on the leg.

"You want one of us to stay around for a while?" Haley asked. "Just in case they decided to make a return trip?"

"Nah, I ain't worried about all that. I think I'm good."

"All right, well, we're gonna go and get started on what we need to do," Recker said. "You need anything else before we get out of your hair?"

"No, like I said, I'm good. Just get these dudes before all this becomes a habit."

"You got it."

Recker, Haley, and Jones left the room and went down to the cafeteria to have a few words with Tyrell's mother and brother. They wanted to make sure Tyrell wasn't making things seem better than they really were. One they were satisfied that everything really was under control there, they left the hospital. As they stood in the parking lot close to their car, they debated their next steps.

"Where to?" Haley asked.

"I figure we got two steps right now," Recker replied. "One is Vincent. The other is Jerome."

"Split up? You take Vincent and I'll take Jerome?"

"Let's take Jerome together. Just in case he has more shenanigans up his sleeve."

**13**

———

Recker and Haley had been watching Jerome's place for about an hour. They didn't know for sure whether he was inside, but judging from the lack of lights on, they assumed not. But they were just going to wait there until he did show up.

"What if this guy's not coming?" Haley said. "What if he took a powder? I mean, if he knows everything that went down, he'd have to be pretty dumb to stick around, wouldn't he? He'd have to know somebody would come looking for him."

"You're assuming he's smart, for one. And two, you're assuming that whoever told him to set this up actually told him what their plans were."

"Yeah, I guess maybe they wouldn't have told him everything."

"It's not likely," Recker said. "They used him for what they wanted him for. They're not gonna tell him everything else. It's just another loose end they'd have to take care of."

"Which they just as easily could do."

"I dunno. I'm thinking not."

"Why?" Haley asked.

"I guess I'm just trying to think like Nowak would. If you're trying to assert control over the city, you need guys on the street, like Tyrell and Jerome, who can get and pass off information to you. Taking them out after they've helped you doesn't really seem like a good strategy to me."

"Yeah, you could be right about that."

"We'll wait a few more hours and see."

They wound up sitting across the street from Jerome's row home until about ten o'clock. Recker saw someone walking up the street in their direction who looked like they fit Jerome's description. Since it was dark out, they couldn't yet see the man's face, but he was short, thin, and had a distinctive walk, almost kind of a swagger, just as Tyrell described him. Recker and Haley jumped out of their car to approach the man. Recker immediately crossed the street to wait by Jerome's house, while Haley started walking down the street in the opposite direction, just in case the man decided to run or do an about-face, Haley would be there to corral him.

As Jerome walked toward his house, he saw the outline of Recker's presence, standing there by the front gate of his neighbor's home. He continued walking toward it, but the hair on the back of his neck started standing up, getting a bad vibe about the situation. Once he finally got to the corner of the block, just before his house, his nerves got the better of him, and he decided to turn around. He turned and saw Haley coming up behind him, not even a block away. Jerome turned his head back around again, and saw Recker moving from his position, walking toward him.

Jerome knew his fears were real at this point and turned the corner, hoping to avoid whoever was waiting for him. Though he wanted to run, an old leg injury prevented him from really running full speed, so he had to settle for a quick walk. Recker and Haley turned the corner also, but weren't running full speed either, wanting to see where Jerome was going. After a few minutes, Jerome was already out of breath, and stopped at the back of a nearby supermarket. He turned around, knowing he wasn't going to outrun these guys, ready to accept whatever fate was coming his way. As the two men approached him, Jerome put his hands out, ready to beg for his life. Recker and Haley cornered him, standing a few feet apart from each other.

"Listen, man, whatever you guys want, you can have it." Jerome started putting his hands in his pockets to rummage for whatever money he had in there. He was quickly stopped.

"You put your hands in your pockets again and I'm gonna assume you're reaching for a gun," Recker said. "And then we won't have anything left to talk about."

Jerome took his hands out of his pockets and made sure he kept them in plain sight. "What do you guys want?"

"Information. That's the game you're in, isn't it?"

"I dunno, man, I just do what I gotta do to survive."

"What about Tyrell? What about his survival?"

"Tyrell? What are you talking about?"

"Tyrell's in a hospital right now fighting for his life because of what you did to him."

"What I did to him? What'd I do? I didn't do nothing. What's he in the hospital for?"

Recker and Haley looked at each other, not sure if they bought the innocent routine yet.

"You told him something was going down at a jewelry store a few days ago, didn't you?" Haley asked.

"Yeah, but that didn't have nothing to do with him."

"Who'd it have to do with then?" Recker asked.

"Listen, these dudes came up to me a few weeks ago and asked if I wanted to make a little extra money."

"Which of course you did."

"Sure, man, who doesn't need a little extra bread."

"And what'd you have to do for it?"

"All I had to do was keep calling everyone I knew for a few weeks, letting them know something was going down at this jewelry store that they told me about. They would tell me when to stop."

"And when was that?"

"About two days ago."

"What about Nowak?"

"Who's that?"

"Tyrell mentioned something about Nowak," Recker said. "I assume you mentioned it to him."

"Oh, yeah, but I didn't know what it meant. When I first talked to them, one of the guys said something about

Nowak, but then the other guy slapped him on the arm like he wasn't supposed to say it or something. I didn't really know what it was supposed to mean."

"These guys, you know who they were?" Haley asked.

"Nah, never seen them before. They put a stack of money down on the table. That did most of the talking as far as I was concerned."

"You must've gotten a name," Recker said. "Somebody to contact or call?"

"Just the one guy, man. His name was uh... Jackson. Yeah, that was it. Jackson."

Recker and Haley immediately looked at each other, both of them recognizing the name as one of Nowak's men. They continued questioning Jerome for a little while longer, but the more they did, the more they realized that he had no idea what was going on. He was just doing what he was told to do and didn't have a clue what was happening beyond that.

"You said Tyrell's fighting for his life?" Jerome asked, seeming concerned for his condition.

"He's gonna make it," Recker said.

"Tyrell's always been good to me. I sure hate to think something happened to him because of me."

"Well, maybe you can make it up to him somehow."

"What could I do?"

"I don't know. That would be up to the two of you to decide. If you want some advice, though, I'd make sure I'd talk to him before he gets out of the hospital."

"Why's that?"

"Because he can't move too well right now," Recker

said. "And if you wait until he gets up and around and moving, and out of the hospital, you may hope that he doesn't find you. At least now you can explain yourself and be assured he won't hit you."

"Yeah, you might be right about that."

"Either that or leave town in the next couple days."

After talking for close to twenty minutes, and convinced Jerome knew nothing more than he was telling them, Recker and Haley finally let the man leave. They stood in the same spot as they watched him walk away and out of sight. They then called Jones as they walked back to their car.

"How did your conversation go?" Jones asked. "Is he still alive?"

"Yes, he's still alive and breathing," Recker replied. "We didn't even put a hand on him."

"Well, that's encouraging. Did you get everything you needed to get out of him?"

"Yeah, he doesn't know much. They pretty much just used him as a stooge. Did and said what they wanted him to for a bag of cash."

"Do we know who?"

"Said a man named Jackson."

"Nowak's man," Jones said, also recognizing the name.

"I think it's pretty safe to say at this point that we were right on target with everything."

"Yes, I would think that's an accurate statement to make at this point. What are you going to do from there?"

"I guess I'm gonna talk to Vincent and let him know we're in the game," Recker said.

Once back in the car, and Recker's conversation with Jones was over, he dialed Vincent's number. Whenever Recker called, it didn't take Vincent long to answer. He was always right on top of it.

"Mike? What do I owe the pleasure of this phone call? Especially at this hour of the evening?"

"Figured we should talk about things," Recker replied.

"Such as?"

"Things I know you don't like discussing over the phone."

"That doesn't really narrow it down too much."

"I'm fine talking about it over the phone if you want, but it involves a certain adversary of yours that's been giving you headaches recently, if that helps to explain things any."

"It does," Vincent said. "You have information that could be useful?"

"I have an offer that could be useful. And some other information too."

"Very well. Sounds like something worth chewing on. Nine o'clock tomorrow? Same place as usual?"

"I'll be there."

"Excellent. Hope that whatever it is will be beneficial to both of us."

"So do I," Recker said.

As soon as Recker put his phone away, Haley wondered how it went. "What'd he say?"

"Meet him at nine o'clock tomorrow morning to discuss it."

"Sounds good. He'll go for it."

"Well there's nothing for him to object to, so I'm sure he will go for it. He's never been one to turn down a present landing in his lap for free. You know, it's kind of funny, even though we've never really had any major problems with Vincent, and we've done good business with him from time to time, every time we do some kind of deal with him, I always feel like I lose a little piece of my soul, you know?"

"Kind of like dealing with the devil, huh?"

"I guess so."

"Didn't they ever teach you on the farm that in order to be a successful agent in the field that sometimes you gotta make a deal with the lesser of two evils in order to catch the more dangerous one?" Haley asked, remembering his time at the CIA training facilities.

"Yeah. But that don't mean we gotta like it."

## 14

Recker arrived at the diner a few minutes before nine o'clock, getting there just ahead of time like he usually did. Also, like usual, Vincent was already there waiting. After walking into the dinner, Recker was greeted by Malloy.

"We're gonna have to stop meeting so often," Malloy said. "I wouldn't want word to get around that we were friends or anything."

Recker grinned. "Yeah. You know, I sure hope you stay on the straight and narrow. I'd hate to have to kill you one day."

Malloy took the good-natured ribbing in his stride. "Assuming you could."

Recker got a laugh out of it and tapped him on the shoulder as he walked past him to go down to Vincent's table. "Stay on the side of the angels, Jimmy. They'll always have your back."

Malloy chuckled, then sat down in his usual spot. Vincent had just finished his breakfast as Recker sat down across from him and washed it down with a sip of orange juice.

"Forgive me for not waiting and offering you something," Vincent said. "But I know you rarely have something, and I was very hungry this morning."

Recker lifted his hand off the table to suggest it was no big deal. "I already ate this morning, anyway."

Vincent smiled, as he often did when he felt like he had some big announcement to share. "Ah, yes, Mia, right? Nothing beats home cooking, correct?" Recker just tilted his head and shrugged to acknowledge the fact. "I'll bet she's a great cook."

Recker nodded. "I'm pretty fond of it."

"I'm sure you are. You know, one day, we'll have to go out to dinner, the four of us, just like regular couples having a night out on the town. Leave our day time troubles behind for an evening."

Recker looked at him strangely. "Four?"

"Yes, I have been seeing someone lately."

"Oh? Serious?"

"Ahh, it could be. You never know how these things will turn out, right? But for now, it looks promising."

"I don't think I've ever even heard you discussing your private life before."

"Well, we can't always be all business all the time, right? Plus, I've been giving some thought to having some kind of legacy. Something to leave behind when it's all said and done. You ever have those thoughts?"

"About leaving behind a legacy?" Recker asked. "No, I can't say that I really have given it much thought."

"Well, I am a few years older than you I believe. You might eventually have those thoughts at some point as well."

"Maybe."

"So, what brings us together here today?"

"Nowak."

"What about her?" Vincent said.

"A couple days ago you asked for my help in going up against her."

"And I recall you said at the time that you weren't interested."

"I guess I've changed my mind."

"Not that I wouldn't be happy and grateful for the change of heart, but why?"

"My reasons are my business," Recker replied.

"Fair enough. It wouldn't have anything to do with a car being blown up in the northeast the other day that I heard about, would it?"

"Not at all. That wasn't me."

Vincent smiled, not positive he was telling the truth or not. "You could understand how I would jump to that conclusion."

"I do. But I was snug in my bed when that thing happened."

"So... about this arrangement? What did you have in mind?"

"I'll help drive her and her gang out of this city. One way or another."

"And in return for this help? What's it going to cost me?"

"Nothing other than it's something to remember for future reference," Recker answered.

Vincent picked his head up and looked away for a second, the grin on his face revealing he didn't believe for a second that this was just out of the kindness of Recker's heart. There was obviously something else going on here, Vincent just didn't know what it was. But with the help that was being offered, he wasn't about to question it either. Whatever Recker's reasons were, they aligned with what was best for Vincent, and that was really all that mattered at the moment.

"So, shall we coordinate efforts?" Vincent asked. "Or do we work independently to accomplish our goal?"

"I think we can just continue what we're doing, going our own ways, and if the need arises for us to come together, then we do it."

"I guess the other question I have is time frame. What are your intentions in regard to that?"

"Now," Recker replied. "I've got other things to work on and I don't intend to let this drag on for weeks or months. My intention is to take her and her group out as soon as possible. Anyone who gets in the way of that... is in my way. How does that align with your time frame?"

"Uh, well, it might be a little quicker than I was imagining, but I'm agreeable to upping my time frame."

"Listen, I'll just come clean, I've gotten word from some sources that in addition to targeting you, she also plans to target me."

"She certainly is planning on going big game hunting, isn't she?" Vincent said with a smile, getting a little amusement in learning he wasn't the only one being targeted. "She has set her sights high. What did you do to earn her wrath?"

"I think it just has to do with our previous encounters with her. I think she just wants to take out whoever she feels could be a threat to her down the line. And she wants to do it now, so she doesn't have to worry about it later."

"I would agree with that."

"What can you tell me about where she is right now?" Recker asked. "Where's she setting up shop these days?"

"That's the million-dollar question right now, isn't it? You think if I knew that I would have been asking you for help the other day? She and the rest of her crew would already be pushing up daisies if that were the case."

"She's gone under?"

"Gone are the days of her setting up shop in comfy hotel suites."

"Any ideas?"

Vincent shrugged, still basically stumped. "I've got guys out, going through the city, trying to pick things up. So far it hasn't turned up anything relevant."

"Can you even narrow it down to an area?" Recker asked.

"Not at this time. We've gotten a few leads that looked promising, then when we investigated further, turned into nothing."

"What about her lieutenants? I know they're out there setting up deals, talking to people."

"They're operating very strategically and stealthily, because we haven't been able to pick up their trail. Their scent is evaporating long before we get there."

The two men sat there silently for a minute or two, both thinking about any other options they could suggest. It really all came down to just finding where Nowak was operating from these days. Until they found that, nothing could be done. Before finishing up their business and going their separate ways for the time being, Recker wanted to bring up Tyrell's situation.

"You heard about what happened to Tyrell?"

By the look on Vincent's face, it was clear he had not. He scrunched his eyebrows together and had a hazy kind of look in his eyes. "I have not. What about him?"

"He was shot. Several times."

"I'm sorry to hear that. When did this happen?"

"Apparently happened last night."

"That's terrible. Is he OK?"

"Looks like he's gonna make it but he'll be out of commission for a little while."

"Any idea who was responsible for the attack?"

"It was Nowak," Recker replied.

"Why? Why target him?"

"I believe she was using him to get to me."

"So, is that your reason for getting involved?"

"No, it goes deeper than that. Even if it hadn't happened, I would still be here having this conversation with you. But it does give me a little extra motivation."

"Understood. So, if I pick up anything on where Nowak might be, I'll fill you in, and I would expect you would do the same?"

"I will."

"Good. There's no need for either of us to do this alone. Together we can be a powerful force the likes of which she has never seen."

Recker wasn't sure about all that bravado, but he didn't really want to argue the point either. All he cared about was getting the job done. They sat and talked a few more minutes before finally going their separate ways.

Once out of the diner, Recker got back in his car and drove off. He pulled over a few minutes later, once he was well out of sight from the diner and pulled out his phone to call Jones.

"I take it you had a nice breakfast," Jones said.

"Don't get cute."

"Did you break eggs together and sing chummy songs?"

"Since when did you get this sarcastic streak in you?"

Jones laughed. "Why should I let you have all the fun?"

"Uh, huh. Anyway, I just finished up."

"And how did it go?"

"Just like we assumed it would," Recker said. "He's not gonna turn down help from us. If either of us get something on Nowak, we'll let the other one know."

"Did he have any new information for us?"

"Nope. Doesn't have a clue where she is."

"Has he been even trying?"

"Yeah, he's gotten some leads, checked them out, they've all come up empty. He's got people out on the street checking, they just haven't turned up anything yet."

"I assume it's going to fall on us then."

"Doesn't it always?" Recker asked.

"Unfortunately. it seems that way."

"Hey, would you want it any other way?"

"I have a feeling my answer will differ from yours."

Recker laughed. "Once again, doesn't it always?"

**15**

———————

They spent the next few days checking what leads they could find, which was admittedly not many. What made it more difficult was that they didn't have Tyrell's eyes and ears on the street. He was as good as there was at finding little nuggets of information. Not having him out there was a big loss for the team. Recker and Jones were in the office, using the computers to try to find a digital trace of any known associate of Nowak's. Haley was hitting the streets, trying to fill Tyrell's void, though he obviously didn't have the same amount of connections. And it showed since he wasn't coming up with anything either.

"I think in the future it might be beneficial to try and create some more contacts on the level of Tyrell, so we're not caught flat-footed again," Jones said.

"Tyrell's on a level all his own. We're not getting anyone else on his level."

"OK. Let me rephrase that. How about, finding anyone, on any level, who can do the things he does, so we're not caught flat-footed again?"

"Problem is if you have too many guys running around doing that, then it's too many and they start running into each other and start fighting with each other for the scoop."

"I'm not talking about having a legion of informants on the street you know, I'm only talking about having one or two more guys."

Recker stopped typing and looked over at his partner strangely. "Weren't you always the guy who wanted to rely less on people and more on your computers? When we started this thing, didn't you try to tell me not to go out on the street and talk as much to cultivate contacts? Wasn't that you?"

Jones rolled his eyes, not liking his words being thrown back at him all these years later, even though they were true. "OK, I may have said that at one time…"

"Actually, I think it was several times."

"I may have thought and said that at numerous points in time, but I have obviously come around to your way of thinking and realized that sometimes you just need eyes and ears on the street. Does that make you feel better?"

"Actually, it does, yeah, just a little."

They continued jabbing at each other for a few more minutes, but after a while, Recker realized that Jones wasn't really paying much attention to him. At first, he just shrugged it off and figured it was just Jones getting wrapped up in his work and not listening anymore. But after listening to Jones mumble to himself, Recker thought he might have come up with something.

"You all right?" Recker asked.

"Wait a minute," Jones said hopefully, just speaking out loud. He didn't even hear Recker's question. "Just wait a minute."

"OK." Recker didn't realize his friend wasn't actually talking to him. After a minute, he got tired of waiting. "What? What is it?"

"Just wait a minute," Jones said, this time hearing Recker speak, though he wasn't listening to his words.

"You already said that. What's the problem?"

Jones finally heard Recker's words this time and snapped his head toward him. "Hmm? Oh, what?"

"Should I just send you an email?"

"What? Why?"

Recker shook his head. "Never mind. Have you come up with something?"

Jones turned back to his computer as he continued reading the information. "I'm not sure."

"Well you must have gotten something. Sounds like you discovered something, unless you were just looking at your family tree or something."

"Uh, I'm not sure yet."

"David, will you stop speaking cryptically and just tell me what you're looking at?"

"Oh. Well, I'm looking at this one property that's been vacant for three or four years now. It's down by the stadiums."

"OK," Recker said. "What about it?"

"Well it's been vacant, like I said, there's a bunch of buildings in there, completely fenced, you know, those high chain-link voltage fences..."

"Yes, I know."

"There's a few buildings in there... none of them connected, you know, their own separate space. I think there's a couple of warehouse type buildings that trucks can back up to for loading purposes, and a few smaller office type buildings... I think four or five buildings in total, set back a distance from the street."

Recker sighed and looked up, frustrated that Jones just spent a few minutes talking without telling him anything. "I know the area, I know the spot you're talking about. What about it?"

"Oh, well, the property was just purchased about three weeks ago."

"So?"

"Well, what's odd is the company that purchased it is virtually unknown."

"New companies form all the time," Recker said.

"But I can't find anything about this company that dates back farther than two months ago when it was formed. I can't find anything else about them. Strange that their first known transaction is a property like that."

"I dunno. Doesn't seem strange to me. If you want to operate a business, you need a place to do it in."

"That's not the only odd thing though," Jones said. "It appears the owners don't have much of a history either. I can't seem to find anything about them prior to them forming the company."

Recker moved his seat closer to Jones so he could take a look for himself. Even if Jones was correct in his suspicions that something was amiss, it didn't mean it had anything to do with Nowak. And it might not have been anything at all. Sometimes people who were well known would buy things under a different company name to disguise who was the true owner for competitive reasons and to get a leg up on their competition.

"So, what are you thinking?" Recker asked.

"I'm not sure yet. I can't find anything related to the building after the sale since then. You would think that new owners, if they plan on using the facilities, usually want to renovate the property to suit them and their business needs. But I can't find any other business accounts that are in their name. Supplies, materials, nothing."

"Could be they're still taking their time."

"Perhaps."

Recker and Jones continued checking the backgrounds on the new owners of record of the property near the sports stadiums. They were still digging an hour later when Haley returned to the office. Jones had gotten him a new vehicle, the exact same as the last one. Same color, make, and style. Haley had gotten used to it and liked it, so he didn't want to move on to something else. He saw his partners working on their computers, but didn't think much of it, and grabbed a drink out of the refrigerator. He sat down on the couch and started drinking, Jones getting a glimpse of him out of the corner of his eye.

"How's the new car working out?" Jones asked.

"Good. But it's the same as the last one so there's really

nothing new to get used to. New model, few new gadgets, basically the same though."

"Glad to hear it."

As Haley continued sipping on his soda bottle, he took a harder look at Recker and Jones. Both of whom seemed to have a little more purpose in their efforts compared to the last time he saw them a few hours ago. They both seemed to be intently looking at things.

"Is there something going on?" Haley asked.

"What do you mean?" Jones replied.

"It just seems like you guys are more... focused on something. Like, a lot more than you were before."

Whenever Recker had his face stuck looking at the computer screen and didn't bother to pick his head up and talk to him, that was usually a good sign for Haley that he was onto something. Otherwise, Recker usually had time for some small talk or joking around with him.

"Oh, well, yes, it looks like we have discovered something," Jones said. "What that is exactly we're not sure yet."

"Well, what is it?"

Recker and Jones alternated in describing what they'd found so far.

"So, you think Nowak's using this place as a base?" Haley asked.

"Very well might be," Jones answered.

Recker was still a bit more skeptical. "We'll see."

"Well, there's only going to be one sure way to find out."

"Sit on it," Haley said, guessing what Jones was inferring.

"Our favorite thing to do," Recker replied.

"When?"

"Might as well do it now."

Recker went over to the gun cabinet and opened it, then closed it quickly without grabbing anything. Jones looked at him strangely and wondered if something was wrong with him.

"Are you all right?"

"Yeah, why?" Recker replied.

"You're not taking extra guns with you? That's very unusual for you. Not that I'm complaining, you understand. Just saying it's unlike you."

Recker smirked, hating to disappoint his friend by doing something against the norm. "Nah, I just remembered I still got a bag of stuff in my car."

Jones rolled his eyes. "Ah, yes, I should've guessed. I don't know what I was thinking. Why on earth would you not have a bag of weapons already in your car?"

Recker laughed. "That's what I said."

Recker and Haley left the office to go down to the property in question, located in South Philadelphia. They took separate vehicles so Recker could keep an eye on the front, while Haley was set up in the back. There was a dedicated entrance in both directions. Each parked along the street, staying back as far as they could so they wouldn't attract attention from anybody going in or out of the property.

"You in?" Recker asked, adjusting his ear piece.

"Yeah, I'm good."

"Anything interesting back there?"

"Nope. You?"

"Negative."

"You really think this is Nowak setting up shop here?" Haley asked.

"I dunno. I have my doubts. But one thing's for sure, isn't it?"

"What's that?"

"She's gotta be setting up shop somewhere."

"Yeah, I'm just not sure this is it."

"Well, we'll find out soon enough," Recker said.

"You get the feeling this is gonna be a long night?"

"These days... they all feel like long nights."

**16**

Recker and Haley sat in their respective spots for three days in a row. They had yet to see any type of movement in or around the property they were staking out. Not a single body went in or out. They were starting to think it was a waste of time.

"How long we gonna keep doing this?" Haley asked.

"I dunno. I guess until we get a better lead to check on."

"Feels like we could be doing more if we were doing something other than just sitting here."

"I hear ya, but there's really not a whole lot else we can do right now," Recker said.

"I suppose not."

Recker could hear the frustration in his partner's voice, and he shared the same concerns, but they really didn't have anything else to work on. Luckily, they didn't have any other cases come up that they'd have to work on and split their time with, because they couldn't just sit there if there were people out there that needed their help. It wasn't until a little after ten o'clock at night that they finally got something. Along the back gate, a car pulled up. A man got out of the passenger side to unlock it.

"Hey, Mike, I got something back here," Haley said, clearly more excitement in his voice.

"What's up?"

"Don't know. Car just pulled up, and a man got out to unlock the gate."

"They go in?"

"Not yet. Guy's just kind of standing around with the gate open."

"He's waiting for somebody I bet," Recker said.

Recker was right on the money. Only a few seconds later, two more cars pulled up, driving right through the opened gates without stopping. As soon as the cars drove through, the other car did as well, and the man waiting by the gate closed it again. He remained standing by it on the inside, though he sat on a nearby chair, near what used to be a guardhouse, trying to remain invisible as he blended in with the darkness.

"Two more cars pulled in," Haley said.

"Recognize anybody?"

"Nah, they were moving too fast, and the windows were tinted. Couldn't really get a good look inside. Nobody got out other than the guy that unlocked the gate and he's too far away to make out too good."

"You able to move in closer?"

Haley squinted his eyes, looking at the front gate, noticing that the man hadn't left his spot.

"Uh, I don't think so. At least not back here. They left a guy by the gate. Maybe I can swing around to the side."

"Just hold your spot for now," Recker replied.

Since all the action seemed to be happening at the back gate, Recker didn't want Haley to move from his position and potentially miss anything else happening back there. Recker looked at the front gate to see if anyone came down to guard it as well. He waited a few minutes but didn't see anyone approach it. Of course, with it being as dark as it was, it didn't mean someone wasn't watching it.

"I'm gonna see if I can get in there," Recker said.

"What are you gonna do?"

"Gonna get out my bolt cutters and get in through the side."

"Anybody by the gate?" Haley asked.

"Can't tell. Don't wanna take any chances."

Recker turned his car on without putting on his headlights and turned down a side street. There was no curb, so he pulled onto a grassy area, just beyond a clump of trees to keep himself hidden. Before getting out, Recker reached into his black bag and removed a pair of small bolt cutters. He got out of his car and hurried over to the fence, not wanting to take too long to get in there.

Recker knelt on one knee and started snipping the bottom of the fence. He cut in a rectangular pattern along the bottom, just big enough that he could slither his way through it. Once he was on the inside, he got back to one knee again, and took out his gun. He took a quick look around, then started running for the nearest building, which was some type of storage unit, while still crouching down to remain unseen. Standing at the back of the building, Recker clung to the wall as he made his way to the side. Once he got around to the front of the building, he peeked around the side, noticing the cars were parked a good distance away.

"How you making out?" Recker heard in his ear.

"I'm on the inside. Getting in closer. Anything else on your end?"

"Negative. Just be careful, they could have as many as twelve guys in there."

Recker slipped around to the back of the building again. There was a little bit of space between the buildings, which would expose Recker's body, but he quickly ran over to it, successful in staying out of sight. He still had to get to a couple more buildings before he was in the vicinity of where the cars were. He sprinted to the next building, and the one after that, making it there unscathed. Recker took a few deep breaths, leaning his back up against the brick building.

"All right, I'm at the building the cars stopped at."

"OK," Haley replied. "If you need help, holler out."

"If I need help, you'll probably know long before I say anything. Just follow the gunfire."

Recker went around the corner, sliding his way up the wall as he made his way to the front. He passed a window and took a peek inside, making sure nobody was in there. Once he got near the front of the building, he poked his head around the corner, not seeing anything in sight, other than the vehicles parked there. Something wasn't right, he thought. Something seemed off.

There didn't appear to be anyone in the cars as he couldn't see any shadows or movement through the front windshields. But as Recker looked around at the nearby buildings, he couldn't see any lights on either. And he doubted they were working or having a meeting in the dark. He could feel the hairs on the back of his neck and arms raise up. They had to be somewhere. He started looking all around, even looking up at the building he was clinging to, thinking that instead of looking for them, maybe they were looking for him.

"Something's not right here," Recker said.

"Why? What's wrong?"

"I can't see anybody. It's like they parked and disappeared. I don't hear voices, lights, nothing."

"Maybe they're having a meeting by candlelight," Haley said with a snicker.

"Yeah, maybe."

The sound of an automatic rifle pierced through the air, Recker ducking and hitting the ground, as the bullets glanced off the brick wall behind him. He quickly got back to his feet and scurried around to the back of the building. He peeked around the corner again, his eyes darting all around, not able to tell where the bullets had come from.

"Mike, you all right?"

"Just stay put for a second," Recker said, not wanting

to get Haley caught up in an ambush. "I can't tell where those shots came from."

"Just remember there's a lot more of them than you."

At this point, Recker was probably closer to the front gate than the back gate, and if he had to go anywhere in a hurry, that's the way he was going. Plus, if he needed to be rescued, it would be quicker for Haley to get to him. Recker slid around to the other side of the building, hoping to pick up a different and better look at whoever was shooting at him. Though it was different, it wasn't better, as he still couldn't see anything.

Recker peeked his head around the corner again and almost got it shot off, as a few more rounds from the rifle fired in his direction. Some of the bullets glanced off the brick, and some just whizzed past his head, Recker ducking once again. Taking a few deep breaths to think clearly, he tried to figure out what was going on. If they knew where he was, they probably had enough men to rush him right there and then. But they weren't. They were sitting back and waiting. The question was why? He then took a quick look to his left, thinking they may have been trying to flank him. They may have been figuring why bother to rush, when they could surround him. He still didn't want to bring Haley in yet until he knew for sure what he was bringing him into. He could try running to the next building, but that was a good sixty to seventy feet away.

Recker slid back down to the back of the building, clinging to the wall. As he turned the corner, a few more bullets rang out. It was a different sound than the others though. This one came from a handgun, fired in rapid succession. Recker took a step back again, his back leaning up against the wall. He was right. They were trying to flank him.

As Recker stood there, deciding on what to do, he put his left hand on his chest and looked down. He didn't put his vest on this time. With all the dreams he'd been having, along with the incident in the alley of the jewelry store, he wished he'd have put it on before coming in there.

"Mike, what's going on in there? You need me to roll?" Haley asked, getting a little jumpy. He didn't like hearing gunfire, knowing what kind of odds Recker was facing, and just sitting there on his hands.

Recker looked around, knowing he was probably going to have to wind up putting Haley in danger too. "Yeah, just wait a minute until I give you the word."

"How you want me to come in?"

"Hot and heavy."

Haley knew exactly what that meant. As soon as Recker gave the word, he'd start his car, rev it up, and crash through the gate, taking on whoever and whatever got in his way. Recker thought about moving back to the front of the building and shooting out some of their tires, but thought better of it, wanting to preserve as much ammunition as possible, knowing the odds weren't in his favor.

As Recker was thinking of his options, a shot rang out from behind him, winging him in the left arm. Recker grunted as he felt the bullet graze his skin, though it was more out of surprise than actual pain. It was actually nothing more than a scratch. Recker quickly turned around and unloaded on the man behind him, having much better aim than he did, killing the guy with three shots to the chest.

Recker ran back to the dead man and turned the corner, ready to engage in a fight, though there was no one else there. He turned around to look at the front where he'd just been, just in time to see the outline of a man holding a gun and pointing it at him. Recker ducked behind the building just as the man fired, the bullets hitting nothing but air for the time being.

Recker knew it was now time to bring in the cavalry. They were surprising him, coming at him in different directions, and they were getting closer. Each bullet seemed like it had his name on it. As much as he didn't want to bring Haley into a bad situation, he had no other choice. He wasn't sure he was getting out of there without Haley's assistance.

"Chris, I could probably use some help now."

"How will I know where you're at?"

"Just keep your headlights on," Recker said. "I'll find you."

"On the way."

Haley was already prepared for battle, having a couple of handguns, along with an automatic rifle sitting on the passenger seat. He turned his car on, then started driving toward the gate, rolling his window down, but not yet turning his lights on. He grabbed one of the handguns, keeping one hand on the steering wheel. Once he got closer to the gate, he turned his headlights on, lighting up the area. He noticed the guard near the gate stand up as he sped towards it. Haley's car crashed through the entrance, knocking the gates wide open, one of which was completely demolished and sent flying into the air.

As Haley sped through the gates, he reached his gun arm out the window, shooting the guard before he was able to get a shot off at him. Haley continued down the path to reach the main buildings, prepared to do a lot of shooting. It was tough to see anything, considering there were no lights on anywhere on the property, but all Haley was concerned about was getting to Recker.

A massive amount of gunfire erupted as the men saw Haley's car come barreling towards them. Hearing the gunfire come from a different area, Recker knew it was Haley coming. He sprinted back to the front of the building, looking out, and seeing the bright headlights from Haley's vehicle. As bullets ripped into Haley's car, looking like it was being turned into swiss cheese, he stopped as he reached the other cars. He grabbed his assault rifle, then jumped out of the driver's seat, and sprayed the cars with bullets, taking out the windows, tires, everything. He was making sure if the men went anywhere, they'd be going on foot.

As Haley took the brunt of the assault at the moment, Recker knew it was his best chance to go. He made a mad dash to the car, the other men recognizing that he was making a break for it. Grass and dirt flew high into the air in every direction as the barrage of bullets hit the ground around Recker's feet. As he got to Haley's car, Recker dropped to the ground and rolled underneath the black SUV until he got to the other side. Haley briefly looked back, seeing his partner had seemingly made it unscathed.

"Nice to see ya!" Haley said.

Recker chuckled. "Yeah, likewise. You got something bigger than this handgun I got?"

"Back seat."

Recker, keeping his head down, opened the back door, immediately seeing an assault rifle on the cushioned seat. He reached in and grabbed it, then dropped back down to the ground, crawling underneath the vehicle for cover. As he took up his position, he could see the flashes from the guns being fired at them, so he knew which direction he was shooting at. After a few minutes of continuous gunfire from both directions, it was clear neither side was gaining the upper hand. And neither seemed interested in advancing their positions at the present time either.

"Mike!" Haley yelled, trying to get the attention of his friend over the booming sounds of gunfire. "Mike!"

Recker couldn't hear him, focused on his targets, as well as the fact that the action was louder than Haley's voice.

"Mike!" Haley yelled again, this time successful in getting his partner's attention since there was a brief lull in the action.

"Yeah?"

"I think we need to get out of here. We're at a standstill here, and if this car takes any more bullets, especially in the hood, getting out of here's gonna be a lot harder than it was getting in."

Recker knew he was right. They weren't progressing in the fight and the odds were too great from where they were to significantly chop them down. If the engine got shot, they were gonna be in a world of trouble, having to get out of there on foot. He crawled out from underneath the car and opened the back door again.

"All right, you drive us out of here," Recker said. "I'll hop in the trunk and open the door. I'll keep on firing to give us some cover until we get out of sight."

"OK."

"What about the guy on the gate?"

"He's out of commission," Haley answered. "Took care of him on the way in."

Haley kept on firing, giving Recker a chance to get in position first. Recker hopped in the back seat, then put the back seats down, that way he could lie down as he fired. He opened the trunk, then let Haley know he was ready to go. Haley stopped firing, then jumped in the car, immediately putting the car in drive. He spun the car around, making a beeline for the back gate. As he drove towards it, Recker kept firing, not so much trying to hit anyone in particular, but more so to try to keep their enemies at bay and keep them ducking, though they kept firing at them as well.

Haley put his foot on the pedal so hard it felt like he almost went through the floor. As Recker kept firing away, Haley revved the engines, quickly speeding up to a hundred miles per hour as they raced toward the back gate. Though they were out of the property's boundaries in less than a minute, every second in a situation like that feels like an eternity.

After speeding along the city streets for a minute, Recker had long since stopped firing since the men were no longer in sight, and Haley finally slowed down, stopping along the side of the road. Recker got out of the car and closed the trunk, then hopped in the passenger seat. As Recker sat down, Haley looked more closely at his friend's arm.

"You all right?"

Recker looked down at his arm, seeing tiny splotches of blood on his sleeve. He moved his arm around in a circular pattern, not really feeling any pain. "It's nothing. Just a scratch. Just grazed me."

"What the hell happened back there?"

"I believe that would be what's referred to as an ambush."

Haley drove around for a few minutes, eventually coming back around the front of the property in order to get to Recker's car. From the front, though they couldn't see too far in, it looked like nothing had ever happened. It was quiet as could be. Haley kept driving until they got to Recker's car, pulling over to let him out. Recker sighed, not able to hide his disappointment.

"You sure you're alright?" Haley asked, seeing his demeanor, not sure if he was more hurt than he was letting on, or if it was just frustration setting in.

"Yeah, I'm good. Let's head back to the office and kick this around a little."

Haley nodded, assuming that's what they would do, anyway. Unless it was extremely late, like after one in the morning, anytime they had a situation, they usually went back to the office to discuss it with Jones. They found it better to talk about things when it was still fresh in their minds. Plus, it was usually hard to sleep right after they'd been in some type of confrontation anyway, since they were often still hyped up from the events.

Before driving away, Haley waited until Recker was in his car and started the engine. Once he did, the two drove back to the office. They let Jones know they had a situation and to be expecting them. Before going, Haley figured it was better to drop his car off somewhere. He didn't think it was a good idea to park his bullet-riddled vehicle in front of their office for everyone to see and question. The office was still located in a small shopping center, with customers constantly coming and going, and it wouldn't take a genius to figure out the car was in some type of firefight.

They eventually wound up taking it to a local mechanic, dropping it off at his garage. They'd used him before and knew he wouldn't ask questions, and more importantly, he wouldn't talk. The mechanic had a small, one-man operation, doing most of the repairs himself. If there was something he couldn't do, or he had more cars than he could handle, he would bring in his cousin, also a shady character in his own right, to help out. For a fee, he didn't mind passing things through inspection that shouldn't be, or clamming up if the police showed up inquiring about a car, or repainting a car that had a little too much heat on it. As long as the money was there, he really didn't care what happened before it got to him.

Recker and Haley then drove to the office after leaving the car at the garage, letting Jones know to call the guy in the morning to let him know it was there. Once they paraded through the office, Jones stopped working as he looked at the pair coming in.

"You two look like a sight," Jones said.

"I feel worse," Recker replied, plopping down on the couch.

Haley took another chair in the corner of the room, a recliner so he could put his feet up to relax.

"So, what happened?" Jones asked.

"It was an ambush, pure and simple," Recker answered.

"How? How could they have known we were there?"

"Well, we were staking the place out for a few days. I have a feeling while we were watching for them, they were somewhere else watching us."

"So, they were just waiting for us to come along?"

"That's how I have it figured. Don't know how else they could've done it."

"Nowak?"

Recker shrugged, believing it was her, though he couldn't prove it. "I dunno. My gut says it was, but I couldn't definitely make anyone out, it was too dark."

"Cars too," Haley said. "Nothing we've come across before."

"It's her MO though. Everything about her, she's

sneaky, she ambushes, that's what she's always done from the minute she rolled into town."

"But that doesn't make proof," Jones said.

"I don't care," Recker replied. "I don't need proof. I know it was her."

"The question is, did she know it was us, or was she just trying to trap whoever she thought was staking out her new place?"

"I don't even care at this point. As far as I'm concerned, she's declared war on us."

Jones noticed the small specks of blood on the sleeve of Recker's shirt. "Did you get hit again?"

Recker didn't even look at his arm this time. "Just grazed my arm. No biggie."

"So, did they purchase this property, assuming that we would find it, hoping that something like this would happen? Or did they have genuine intentions on using, then noticed they were being watched, and decided to make the most of it?"

"I have a hard time believing that they'd use the place again after this. Then again, they paid a lot of money for the property, didn't they?"

"They did."

"Be an expensive ambush."

"Especially one that didn't work," Haley said.

"Must be aiming to do something with it."

# 17

Over the next few days, Recker and Haley took turns driving by the property that they assumed Nowak bought. Assuming that they'd been watched the last time they were there, they were uncomfortable staking the place out again, especially knowing that they didn't realize they were being watched before. But this time, they'd just drive by to see if someone was there, or they'd sit and park for a few minutes before moving on. The back gate wound up getting repaired two days after Haley busted through it.

Recker and Haley had just gotten back to the office after taking care of an intended robbery of a convenience store. Jones was at the refrigerator getting a bottled water when they came in the door.

"How'd it go?" Jones asked.

"Piece of cake," Haley answered.

"Couple of young kids," Recker said. "Scared out of their minds."

"Was that before or after you showed up?" Jones asked.

"Both."

Jones took his water and walked back to his desk to sit down.

"Find out anything useful yet?" Recker asked.

"In regard to?"

"Nowak."

"I did find one interesting thing," Jones said, shuffling a few papers around until he found the one he was looking for. "I found a manifest for our mysterious property, scheduled to be delivered tomorrow."

"So, they're planning on moving in. What'd they order?"

"Says office furniture."

"Office furniture?"

"That's what it says."

"I can't make heads or tails out of this," Recker said. "I wish this lady was more straightforward instead of deviously planning everything."

They sat around for a little while, stewing about the situation, though it was mostly Recker doing the agonizing, as Jones and Haley got on computers to work. About an hour went by, and Recker had finally gotten up and started moving around, though it was mostly just pacing around the office. Though his marching around the office didn't usually bother Jones, for some reason, in this instance, it was distracting.

"Are you planning on wearing out the carpet?" Jones asked.

"Possibly."

"Why don't you try sitting down and doing something productive?"

"I am doing something productive," Recker answered.

"I fail to see it."

"Maybe you're not looking hard enough."

"Michael, just sit down and relax."

Recker was about to continue debating, but his phone started ringing. He was surprised to see it was Malloy calling.

"Something I can do for you?" Recker asked.

Recker immediately pulled the phone away from his ear, shocked to hear the sound of gunfire going off in the background.

"You butt-dialing or are you busy?" Recker said.

Jones and Haley both stopped what they were doing and looked over at him, his choice of wording getting their attention. As Recker waited for a response, he could hear more gunfire in the background. It sounded like a war was going on. Not knowing what was going on, but assuming there were problems, he patiently waited for Malloy to respond.

"You there?" Malloy said, after shooting off a few more rounds.

"Yeah. What the hell is going on there?"

"We got suckered. Need your help fast."

"Where are you?"

"Old supply building off of the boulevard. Says

Bowman's on a big sign on the front of the building. You know it?"

"Yeah, I know it."

"I don't know how much longer we can hold out."

"Who and what are you up against?" Recker asked.

"Nowak's crew. We're outnumbered, bunch of my guys are dead, the rest of us are likely to join them if we don't get some kind of help."

"OK, sit tight, we'll get there as soon as we can."

"Hurry up 'cause we're running out of bullets too."

Recker hung up and stuffed the phone in his pocket. He motioned to Haley to drop what he was doing and follow him. "C'mon, we gotta go."

Haley jumped out of his chair. "Where we going?"

Jones spun his head around, wondering what was going on. "Where are you two going? Who was that? What's happening?"

Recker and Haley grabbed a few more guns out of the gun cabinet and raced toward the door. He tried to explain as much as he could before leaving. "Not sure. Malloy and his men got ambushed by Nowak in some factory off the boulevard. Says they're outnumbered and running out of ammo. Thinks he ain't got much time left if we don't get there to help."

"At least give me the address so I can pull it up on the satellite so I can advise you what you're walking into."

"Called Bowman's," Recker said, his voice trailing off as he and Haley ran down the steps.

Jones got up and closed the door, which was still swinging open. He then went back to his computer and brought the image of the building on his computer screen. He didn't like the fact that Recker and Haley left so quickly without knowing what they were walking into, but there wasn't much he could do about that. He could try to bring up images of the place so he could direct them to the best spot to enter the building though.

Recker and Haley got to Bowman's in about twenty-five minutes, seeing a bunch of cars parked in the lot in front. A few of those he recognized as vehicles that belonged to Vincent's crew. They kept driving, parking in the building next to it, which was a large car dealership. Once they parked, they jumped out of the car, each armed with a couple of pistols, as well as an automatic rifle. They weren't sure what they were walking into, but they were going to be well armed for it.

Before they got there, Jones got the schematics for the building and let them know to enter along the side. There wasn't a door there, but a circular ladder that led up to a third-floor window. They assumed that the front and back doors would be guarded, so they hoped going up a side ladder would be the path of least resistance. After leaving the protection of all the new cars on the lot, Recker and Haley scurried to the side of the former medical supply factory.

Recker quickly climbed up the ladder as Haley provided a lookout from down below. If anyone showed their face in the window before Recker got there, Haley would shoot it off. Once Recker got to the window without incident, Haley started climbing as well. The window was locked shut, but Recker took his rifle, which was hanging by the strap around his back, and spun it around, breaking a small piece of the glass. Haley heard the glass break and looked up, moving his head to the side as the pieces fell down past him.

Recker put his hand through the hole in the window to unlock it, pushing it up. He climbed through it and spun around, looking for the first sign of trouble. It was dark, but it looked like he was in some type of storage room. At least it used to be. It wasn't much now but a lot of trash and empty boxes littered on the floor. He walked over to the door, waiting until Haley got in. Recker opened it a slither and immediately heard shots being fired. He could tell they weren't coming from the floor they were on as they sounded a little muffled.

Once Haley had entered through the window, Recker opened the door further, and stepped out. They ran down the hallway, ready to join the fight, without having a clear plan in mind. There was an elevator to their right and the stairs to their left. Haley grabbed Recker's arm, having an idea.

"What?" Recker asked, wondering why he had stopped moving.

"I got an idea how we can get them by surprise."

"I would think just showing up would accomplish that."

"No, but what if we send the elevator down there?" Haley said. "They'll hear it coming, think that maybe they got company, then everyone's attention will be looking at that. Meanwhile, we come in the back way and go down the stairs."

"And hopefully catching them with their backs turned."

"That's the idea."

"Might work," Recker said. "Worth a shot."

Haley ran towards the elevator, as Recker ran over to the stairs. As Haley pushed the button for the first floor, Recker started making his way down the steps. Haley then ran over to the stairs as well. Recker had just turned the corner on the stairwell when he ran into another man, who was making his way up. Recker knew all of Vincent's men by now. He knew their names, their faces, and the cars they drove. This guy wasn't one of them.

The man was surprised at the sight of Recker, and having a gun already in his hand, brought it up to try to use it. Recker was too fast for him though. He lifted his rifle up, and with both hands on the weapon, fiercely jabbed it at the man's face, stunning him and knocking him off balance. The man fell backwards, his gun flying out of his hand, as he rolled down a couple of the steps. The man was bleeding heavily from his nose, which was definitely broken from the blow. He wasn't out of the fight yet though. In spite of the fact that he was a little groggy, he still attempted to get back to his feet. Knowing his weapon was too far away to do him any good now, he was ready to duke it out with the intruder. As Recker walked down a couple more steps, not an ounce of panic or excitement in him, he approached the man once more. Recker ducked a right hand, then delivered another blow with his weapon, this time striking the side of the man's face.

While in most circumstances, Recker would've put a few bullets in the man by now, ending his miserable existence, he couldn't afford to have the shot be heard. Instead, he walloped the man a few more times in the face until he was knocked unconscious. As he stepped over the laid-out man, Haley came flying down the steps, hearing some type of commotion. Once he saw the man lying there, he then shot Recker a look.

"The welcoming committee," Recker said.

"Did he give you a proper welcome?"

"No, but I gave him one."

The two of them proceeded down the rest of the steps, keeping an eye out for anybody else on the way. Nobody else was on the stairwell, though, and they got down to the first floor unimpeded. They looked through a small oval piece of glass on the door that led to the first floor, seeing several men shooting their weapons. They had a direct view of the other side of the room, where the elevator was located. Recker, seeing the light on the elevator indicate it was passing the second floor, put two fingers in the air to signal to his partner where it was at the moment. Recker kept his hand in the air, putting up his index finger as soon as the elevator landed on the first floor.

Both men got their weapons ready, holding their rifles out in front of them, ready to barge through the door. The elevator dinged, causing alarm and confusion from the men on the floor. The men inside started yelling and pointing, assuming they were about to have company, as they knew none of their men would be using the elevator.

The gunfire had come to a sudden stop as everyone's attention was drawn to the elevator, just as Haley hoped it would.

Before opening the door and announcing their presence, Recker put his arm out and pointed to his right, indicating that all their targets were on the right-hand side once they entered the room. Several of the men inside had advanced toward the elevator in order to check it out.

"It's empty!" one of the men shouted.

"What do you mean it's empty?!"

The man threw his arms up, unsure what else he could say. "It's empty."

"It didn't just start itself!"

"What do you want me to tell ya? It's empty."

"Somebody go check upstairs and see if we got company!" the leader of the group ordered. "Somebody might be playing games with us."

Recker nodded at Haley, letting him know he was about to go. He threw open the door, and he and Haley burst through it.

"No games here," Recker said, getting an eye on all his targets.

Surprised at the sight of them, knowing exactly who Recker and Haley were, the men were caught off guard. Recker and Haley wasted no time in firing their weapons. They immediately mowed down four men directly in front of them, including the man who checked the elevator, as well as the leader of the group. Though they'd gotten the jump on them, Recker and Haley knew they couldn't just stand there in the open, as there still seemed to be four or five men left, hiding behind some crates and boxes.

Recker looked behind them as he continued firing, noticing Malloy crouching down behind a crate, right up against the wall. Malloy waved at him, motioning for them to join him at his spot. Recker tapped Haley to follow him as the two men retreated to the back of the room. Haley kept firing as Recker got the rundown on what had happened so far.

"Nice to see you could make it," Malloy said.

"I'll send you a bill in the mail for our services."

Malloy laughed, his mood getting much better at finally seeing some backup arrive. "It's a bill I'd gladly pay."

"So, what happened?"

A few shots ripped into the wall behind them, cutting their conversation short.

"Shoot first, talk later," Malloy said.

Recker and Malloy joined Haley in firing towards the remaining men. After a few minutes, it appeared neither side was gaining an advantage, and likely wouldn't unless one side decided to take a chance in moving forward. Considering the lack of objects to hide behind, no one decided it was worth the risk. There was an opening along the far wall, closer to where their would-be victims were, and the men decided it was safer to leave the premises and live to fight another day, instead of putting themselves in further danger by continuing to fight.

To give themselves a better chance at escaping safely,

the men fired a barrage of bullets, not really caring if they hit Recker and company, but just hoping it would cause them to duck for cover, that way they wouldn't get shot as they ran. Their plan worked, as Recker, Haley, and Malloy ducked to avoid being shot, the men ran through the opening, which led to a small receptionist area and the front door. Malloy was too tired from the battle to pursue them any further, though Recker and Malloy both ran after the men, hoping to pick one or two more of them off before they left. Unsuccessful in their attempts, after they observed the men fleeing in an unmarked white van, Recker and Haley came back to the room all the fighting had occurred in.

Malloy was just leaning up against the wall, checking his weapon, and putting the last clip he had into his pistol. Recker and Haley looked around at all the damage, counting eight dead bodies on the floor. Three of them they recognized as men of Vincent's crew. The other five were from Nowak's bunch, four of whom Recker and Haley gunned down. Malloy also looked down at his fallen comrades and sighed, upset at losing them. They were good men, loyal, could be counted on, and never backed down from a fight. He considered them friends.

"So, what happened?" Recker asked.

"Got a tip."

"Anonymous?"

"Yeah," Malloy said with a laugh, though not finding it amusing. "Said they knew a place that Nowak was doing business in. Said she was using it as storage for her drug stash."

"So, you guys came down here to check it out?"

"Yeah. We sat on it for a couple hours, didn't see anyone coming or going, and it didn't look like the place was being used."

"So, you came in to investigate?"

Malloy nodded. "Everything was cool at first. Checked every floor, didn't find anything. Chalked it up to a bad tip. Once we were done looking everything over, we were just about to leave, then a bunch of men came out of nowhere. Started chopping us up. Nothing else we could do. We were backed up, cut off, couldn't escape anywhere. Figured the best thing I could do at that point was call you."

"I know the feeling."

"What do you mean?"

"Few days ago, they tried the same thing with us," Recker answered. "They bought some old warehousing property down in South Philly. We sat on it for a few days, then saw some activity, so I went in."

"They were waiting for you?"

"Yep. Chris had to barrel in there and bail me out."

"Seems to be a pattern," Malloy said.

"Yeah. A good one too. They're good at sneaking around and ambushing people."

"Too good."

"Either that or we're getting sloppy at falling for it."

"Probably a little of both."

"Might be right about that," Recker said.

Malloy let his eyes return to his fallen friends on the floor. "Hate to just leave these guys here."

"Nothing else you can do for them."

"Yeah, guess you're right."

"Best you can do for them now is claim their bodies when they hit the morgue, give them a good funeral."

"What are we gonna do about Nowak?" Malloy asked. "She's becoming a real pain in the ass."

"I dunno. Maybe it's time we gave her a taste of her own medicine."

**18**

———

Recker and Haley had spent most of the morning double checking the known places Nowak was known to have frequented. The Bowman's factory was now a crime scene and inhabited by the police and detectives investigating, the warehouse facility in South Philadelphia didn't seem to be occupied, and they had run out of leads. They had

no sooner stepped foot in the office when Recker's phone rang, Vincent on the other end of the line.

"Yeah?" Recker said.

"First of all, I'd like to thank you for helping Jimmy out last night. It's quite likely without your interference that he would no longer be with us."

Recker didn't particularly care about being thanked. The only thing he did care about was getting rid of Nowak once and for all. "You can thank me when this is over."

"In regard to that, Jimmy mentioned you said something about turning the tables on her, giving her a taste of her own medicine."

"Yeah, but it was just a thought," Recker said. "Doesn't much matter if we don't know where she is."

"Once we do, I would suggest that we no longer do anything independently of each other. It's obvious what they're trying to do. The next time either of us get any type of lead or tip on their whereabouts, I suggest we act on it together. Together we're stronger."

"Yeah, I would agree with that."

"Do you have any other leads at the moment?"

"Not right now," Recker said with a sigh. "We just took a drive past the last two locations we both got ambushed at and there's nothing there."

"It seems they're stepping up their plans. Things are starting to happen much quicker now. I would think it won't be too long before they enact the next stage of their production."

"Might be right about that."

As they continued discussing plans, Haley went over to the desk and sat next to Jones. Seeing what he was working on, Haley jumped right in to help. After a few minutes, Haley suddenly stopped, an idea coming into his head. Looking at the computer screen, though not focusing on it, he put his hands up and started moving them around as if he was talking to someone. Jones noticed the gyrations and froze his hands above the keyboard, just as he was about to come down on it and turned his head to look at him. Jones continued looking at him for a moment, wondering why Haley was acting so strangely. Haley kept going with his hand motions, but now was also moving his lips, whispering something, though not loud enough for Jones to actually make out what he was saying. After a few more minutes, Jones couldn't remain silent any longer. He was too curious to let Haley continue.

"May I ask what it is that you're doing?" Jones asked.

Haley didn't respond at first, still deep in thought. After a delayed reaction, he then answered, realizing something was said. "Hmm?"

"I noticed you seem to be having a conversation with yourself. Are you developing some new kind of code or something?"

"What? No."

"Would you like to clue me in to your strange behavior?"

"Oh, I was just thinking," Haley replied.

"I kind of assumed as much. Would you like to get into more specifics?"

"Well, I was thinking of how we can turn the tables on Nowak."

"And have you come up with anything?"

"Uh, I dunno, I might have."

Jones' shoulders slumped, hating to have to draw the information out of him. It almost was if he was talking to Recker. "Chris, please don't turn into Michael."

"What do you mean?"

"Because for as long as I've known him, I would say over ninety percent of the time, what could be answered in about a minute, it takes him ten times as long. It's as if I have to reach down inside him, grab whatever information he's holding, then bring it out of his body for me to know what he's thinking about. Please don't turn into that."

Haley laughed. "I'll try not to."

"I would be forever grateful. So, now, let's try this again. Would you care to explain what it is that you're deciphering over there?"

"It's like I said. What can we do to turn the tables?"

"So far the answer to that is nothing," Jones replied.

"Not so. So far, everything that we've uncovered, hasn't led to anything, or it's led to some sticky situations. But there's one thing at our disposal that we haven't tried. That we already know has a tie-in to Nowak's crew."

"And what would that be?"

"It's not a what. It's a who."

Jones thought for a second as to who he was referring to, but all he was drawing was a blank. "I'm not seeing it."

"Jerome."

"Jerome?" Jones asked, not seeing as how he could help. "I fail to see the connection."

"He's got a line to Milton, right?"

"I'm sure that's a lead that is long since dead. They used Jerome for their own purposes. I'm sure they no longer have any communication with him."

"But what if he communicates with them?" Haley asked, still a slight grin on his face, thinking his ploy could and would work. "What if he tells them something about us? About how we'll be somewhere, wherever we decide, and we set up a trap for them?"

Jones gave a slight shake of his head as he thought about it, unsure this plan could work. "They're not going to listen to him."

"Why not? They apparently thought enough of him to work with him once. And he came through for them. There's no reason to think they wouldn't again, not if the tip was juicy enough."

As they continued to debate the specifics of such a plan, Recker finished his conversation with Vincent. He came over to the others and plopped down in a chair, tossing his phone on the desk. Jones and Haley stopped their discussion as they turned their attention toward Recker.

"How is Vincent?" Jones asked.

"Frustrated."

"Aren't we all?"

"He sounds as down about everything as I can ever recall," Recker said. "He doesn't know what to do. Nothing's working. Informants aren't giving him anything. Staking places out has gone nowhere. Acting on the tips he has gotten hasn't led to anything. It's frustrating."

"Well, I guess he has joined the club."

Jones happened to glance at Haley, who was giving him a look of his own, while nodding his head. He still had that smirk on his face. Jones rolled his eyes, then threw his hands up.

"Why not?" Jones said.

Recker looked at him strangely, then at Haley as he tried to figure out what was going on. "You wanna get into that?"

"Chris thinks he may have an idea, though I still have plenty of doubts as to the validity of it."

"Might as well hear it. More than we got going on right now."

Haley opened up about his plan, giving a few more details than he originally gave to Jones. After listening to his presentation, Recker seemed on board with the idea.

"Let's do it," Recker said, mere seconds after Haley finished talking.

Jones was stunned, not only that he agreed to it, but that he did it so soon, without even putting a lot of thought into it. "Are you serious?"

"Why not?"

"You barely even gave it a second thought."

"So?"

"So, since when did you agree to things so haphazardly?"

"It's not haphazard," Recker answered. "It's taking an honest look at things and determining that we don't have anything else going on at the moment. Why not take a stab at it?"

"Seems very unlike you."

"Why are you so against it?"

"It's not that I'm against it," Jones replied. "It's just that I have my doubts about it working."

"Well, I'm looking at it like this. Sometimes if you throw crap against the wall... sometimes it sticks."

"That's not exactly sound strategy."

"Didn't say it was," Recker said. "Just that sometimes it works."

"All right, since you two are gung-ho on this, where do we begin?"

Recker looked at Haley since it was his plan.

"Let's talk to Jerome," Haley said. "If he's really serious about Tyrell and upset at being played, then he'll want to help."

Jones couldn't help but continue to be a Debbie Downer. "Even if you are correct and Jerome gets hold of Milton, or anybody else from that crew, they are going to be on extremely high alert. Don't you think that they're going to be on the lookout for some type of... revenge or set up or something?"

"Probably. That's why we're going to have to do it in two stages."

"Two stages?"

"It's like you said, they're initially gonna wonder about it," Haley replied. "But they can't afford not to at least check out whether it's accurate or not."

Recker now knew exactly what Haley had in mind. "So, the first time will be them making sure he's not making things up or setting them up."

"Exactly. Then when the second tip comes along, they'll figure it's definitely on the level, and they'll roll on it."

"And that's when we get them. On the second go-round."

"That's the plan," Haley said.

Though Jones still had his doubts, he nonetheless got on board. He figured if his partners had high hopes of the plan succeeding, who was he to be the stick-in-the-mud?

"What if Jerome's left town?" Jones asked.

"He hasn't," Recker answered. "He wanted to try and make it up to Tyrell."

"What if that didn't go over well?"

"Only one way to find out. Ask."

Recker grabbed his phone again and called Tyrell.

"Hey, I assume you didn't die from the hospital food yet."

"Hey, man, let me tell you, this hospital food ain't all that bad," Tyrell replied. "I know all the jokes about hospital food, but it's really not bad. Especially the mashed potatoes... mmm, they are sweet!"

Recker laughed. "Maybe you should get shot more often. Least you get some free meals out of it."

"No way, I'll leave the getting shot to you. The food ain't bad, but I sure don't wanna stay."

"How much longer they keeping you?"

"Ahh, couple more days. Just wanna make sure everything's good before they release me."

"Listen, did Jerome ever get in touch with you?"

"Yeah, he dropped by a couple days ago," Tyrell answered. "Apologized for everything, said he was a fool and got played."

"You accept?"

Tyrell sighed. "Yeah, I guess so. I'm a sentimental type of guy, man. I mean, I've known him a long time. As much as I really wanted to kick his ass, I mean, it's the world we live in, you know?"

"I do."

"Things happen. People make mistakes. As long as

they own up to, accept it, you gotta move on. What else can you do?"

"I hear ya. That brings me to why I called."

"What, you mean you didn't call just to shoot the breeze?" Tyrell said with a laugh, knowing full well that he didn't.

"Not this time. It's about Jerome."

"What about him?"

"If things are cool between you two, I imagine he's sticking around?"

"As far as I know. Why?"

"There's something we wanna try," Recker said. "We think we can use him to get to Nowak. At least that's the plan. You think he would help with that?"

"Well, he said he was gonna make all this up to me somehow, so yeah, I think he would help. I mean, as long as you're not sending him in to a firing squad or nothing."

"No, nothing quite that dramatic. Just using him to pass on bad information."

"Then I think he's your man. You really think he's gonna be able to get to Nowak's crew though?"

"Got to them once before."

"That was then. This is now."

"All we can do is give it a shot."

"Yeah, well, let's hope it works," Tyrell said. "Getting tired of all this nonsense. You get shot, I get shot, Chris gets his car blown up, what's this world coming to nowadays?"

Recker laughed. "Not safe for man nor beast out there."

"You got that right. Man, we gotta get Nowak out of this city. She's making it an unsafe place to live."

"As opposed to before?"

"Hey, at least nobody was getting blown up, and I was never in the hospital. Pretty soon she'll be having us all call the cops for protection," Tyrell said, laughing at his own joke.

"You must be on some pretty strong drugs there."

"Yeah, whatever it is, it ain't enough."

"I bet."

"Hey, you make sure you get this woman. She gives all of us a bad name."

"You got my word on that," Recker said. "One way or another, we'll get her."

Recker was standing by the edge of the building, looking at the back door of the jewelry store. It was cold and raining. He tried calling Haley to see where he was, but he got no answer. The phone just kept on ringing. After he put it away, it started ringing again. But it wasn't Haley though. It was Mia. It was strange, Recker thought. She never called him when she knew he was out working on something.

"Yeah? You OK?" Recker asked.

"I just wanted to make sure you're wearing your vest," Mia replied. "It's dangerous out there. I don't want you getting hurt."

Recker looked down at his chest, but the vest wasn't there. He must have forgotten to put it on.

"I'll be fine," Recker said.

"You always say that."

"Because it's true."

"You better be right. You better come back to me."

*"I always will."*

*Just as he muttered the words, the back door to the jewelry store flung open, a gang of thieves stepping out. There were seven of them, all wearing masks, and carrying assault rifles. Recker quickly hung up and put the phone back in his pocket as he readied himself to stop the gang from fleeing the scene. Recker jumped out from beyond the building, in plain view of everyone, and started firing his gun. The other men dropped white sacks of merchandise and began doing the same. After a few minutes, the men were just too much for Recker to over-come. Recker's chest was soon riddled with bullets as he was knocked off his feet. His gun flew out of his hand as he lay there on his back, motionless. His eyes flickered as they began to feel heavy. He could barely feel the rain now as the life inside him felt like it was draining out of the numerous holes in his chest. His eyes became too heavy to stay open any longer, and they closed for the final time.*

Recker jumped up in his bed, breathing heavily, the nightmare seeming all too real. He looked down at his chest and put his hand on it, making sure there were no holes there. Sweat was pouring off his face, and he wiped his head with his forearm. He then shivered, trying to shake loose the all-too vivid images from his memory. Mia could feel him moving around and also woke up. As soon as she saw him sitting there, sweating, shivering, and looking rattled, she knew what happened. She put her hands on his back, resting her head against his shoulder. When Recker felt her touch, he turned his head, putting his against hers.

"How bad this time?" Mia asked.

"Same as the others. This one felt the most real though."

"What happened?"

Recker hesitated, not sure if he wanted to remember it. But then he thought maybe it would be therapeutic. "I was at the jewelry store again. Same situation. But Chris wasn't there this time."

Mia had a feeling she knew how it was going to go but stayed silent so as not to interrupt.

"Just before they came out, you called and told me to make sure I had my vest on. But I didn't have it. Then they came out and we got into a fight. Next thing I know I'm on the ground, dying."

"It's just a dream," Mia said, rubbing his back.

"It felt so real."

"It doesn't matter. It's all in your head."

"They feel like they're getting worse," Recker said.

"Maybe you should talk to somebody. A psychiatrist or something."

"And tell them what? That I'm the famous Silencer that runs around knocking everybody off?"

"They're doctors, they have confidentiality agreements. I'm sure you're not the first person they've treated that's been on the opposite side of the law or done something..."

"No, I can't. Whatever it is, I'm just gonna have to figure it out on my own."

Though Mia didn't like that answer, and wished he would talk to someone about it, she had to respect his wishes. Recker was right, the dreams did seem to be getting worse with each passing week. They became more vivid and they lasted longer. It seemed his incident at the jewelry store only made them worse. But even though Mia wanted him to get help, she knew she couldn't force him, and she couldn't keep nagging him about it. If she kept bringing it up, Recker would just close himself off. That's just how he was. And she didn't want that. She wanted him to at least be able to confide in her, if no one else.

Mia looked at the time and saw it was three o'clock. While she would have been willing to stay up the rest of the morning to help Recker through his problems, she thought it would be best if he tried to go back to sleep. She didn't want him, in his current state, to be out somewhere on a dangerous assignment and be tired. He would be lethargic, and his decision making might be slowed, making one of those nightmares become a reality. At least if he was fresh, he would think and act more clearly.

"C'mon, let's go back to bed," Mia said, pulling him down beside him, putting her arms around him as he put his head on her chest.

"I'm not sure I want to."

"Just relax and close your eyes," Mia said in a warm, soothing voice. "Just think of something pleasant. Just think of us. Don't think of anything else. Just us."

Her comfortable and gentle embrace did the trick, as Recker drifted off to sleep a short time later. They didn't wake up again until eight o'clock, with Recker having a peaceful sleep the second time around. He looked over at

Mia, who was still lying next to him, and was staring at him. Recker leaned over and gave her a tender kiss.

"Thank you for helping me last night."

Mia gave him one of those beautiful smiles of hers. "Anything for you. I do wish you'd talk to someone about it. And I'm not gonna keep pestering you about it. That's all I'll say about it."

"Just talking about it with you is good enough. You help me more than anyone else could."

They spent the next hour getting dressed, eating breakfast, and just talking, though not much of Recker's problem. He didn't like being the focus of attention and quizzed Mia about what was going on at the hospital. Once nine o'clock came around, Recker knew he should be leaving, as he was already later than he usually was, but had a hard time tearing himself away from Mia.

"Shouldn't you be going soon?" Mia asked, also observing the time.

"Trying to get rid of me?"

"Never. But you're almost always gone by now."

Recker shrugged. "There's nothing really pressing. Don't really have to be anywhere until later."

They started kissing but were quickly interrupted by the sound of Recker's phone, which was often a mood killer.

"Saved by the bell again," Mia sarcastically said.

Recker pulled out his phone and answered it without looking to see who it was. "Yes?"

"Rise and shine, sleepyhead," Jones kidded.

"I'm not sleeping."

"Oh, are you planning on playing hooky today?"

Recker rolled his eyes at Jones' sense of humor. "No, I'm coming."

"Before lunch? Should I roll out the red carpet for you?"

"Is there something that's breaking and urgent?"

"No."

"Then why are you calling me and breaking my stones?"

"I guess because it's fun."

"So glad I'm here for your amusement," Recker said.

"All kidding aside, you're usually here by now, is everything all right?"

"Everything's fine."

"Because you're usually here around eight-ish. And it's now after nine."

"I'm aware of the time. I learned to tell it a long time ago."

"Just checking to make sure you didn't run into some type of problem on the way in."

"No, I just haven't left yet. I'm coming though."

"Oh. Is Mia there with you?"

"She does live here you know."

"Well I wasn't sure if she was at work yet."

"No, she's got a mid-shift."

"Say no more," Jones said, beginning to understand why he wasn't there yet. "Sorry to interrupt you two love-birds. Just try to conserve some energy. Remember, you were talking to Jerome later."

"Nothing's going on here."

"Uh, I don't need to hear any details."

"David..."

"Just get in when you're ready."

"David..."

Jones hung up, not wanting to interrupt the couple any longer in case they were busy. Recker shook his head as he put the phone back in his pocket.

"Everything OK?" Mia asked.

Whenever Jones called with an important task, Recker usually got a certain look on his face, and his mannerisms changed. She could always tell when something was up. But he didn't display any of those characteristics this time.

"Yeah, just David being a smartass."

"David?" Mia said, her face indicating that she didn't believe it.

"Yeah, he does have his moments. Not many of them, but he has a few."

Mia then threw her arms around Recker's neck. "Guess you have to go soon?"

Recker sighed, not really wanting to, but knowing he had to get moving at some point. "Yeah, I guess I should, huh?"

"Have anything extremely dangerous going on today?" Mia asked, still concerned about Recker's mental state, and throwing himself into a bad situation.

Recker smirked. "Nothing too dangerous. Not extremely anyway."

"Just promise me you'll be very careful if something comes up."

"I will."

"And don't second guess yourself, thinking about the nightmares you've been having. They're not real. They don't indicate anything." Recker smiled and nodded. Mia then planted another kiss on his lips. "And please wear your vest."

**20**

___

R ecker and Haley were waiting outside Jerome's house, the same as they did the last time they were there. They'd been waiting for over an hour, getting there early to make sure that nobody else was staking out the place either. And they wanted to wait for nightfall to try to conceal their meeting under the cover of darkness. They wound up waiting a little longer than they had planned, not seeing a sign of Jerome for over two hours. Once they did, and they knew they were alone in waiting for the informant, they got out of their car to approach him.

Just like the last time they talked to Jerome, Recker went by the front gate to wait, while Haley walked down the street so he could then cross over and come up behind him. Once Jerome got closer to his house, he saw the outline of a man waiting by his home again. Due to the darkness, he couldn't yet tell who it was. But he always erred on the side of caution. And Jerome's first inclination was always to run. Well, a light jog or walking quickly in his case due to his leg. But in any event, his mind was just telling him to get away. Far away.

Jerome got to the corner of the street and turned, going down the side street. Recker and Haley quickly pursued him, with him finally stopping once he got to the back of the supermarket. Just like last time.

"Well this seems familiar," Recker said, noticing the pattern.

"Oh, it's you guys again," Jerome said, finally recognizing his pursuers.

"You might wanna think up a new exit strategy for when you want to elude someone," Haley said.

"Yeah, I'll have to work on that. What do you guys want? If it's about Tyrell again, man, I already talked to him, him and I are cool."

"It's not about Tyrell," Recker said.

"Then what's it about?" Jerome asked, starting to look nervous about their intentions.

"We're here for you."

"Awe, c'mon, man, I already told you guys it wasn't my fault. I wasn't trying to hurt you guys, really, I wasn't. They duped me into all that."

"Relax, we're not here to work you over."

"You're not?"

"No. We just want your help. And considering everything that's happened we figured you might wanna help us too."

"Like what'd you have in mind?"

"We want you to get in contact with the same man you did before."

"Huh?" Jerome said, scratching his head, looking confused.

"You may have gotten back into Tyrell's good graces, but you haven't gotten back into ours. And if you want us to forget your role in everything that's happened, then we want you to do a few things for us."

Jerome looked uncomfortable, getting the feeling he was being railroaded. But he also didn't want to be in the bad graces of The Silencer. And he also felt that he probably owed them one for getting suckered the way he did by Nowak's crew.

"OK. Say I'm on board, what exactly you want me to do?" Jerome asked.

"I'll give you specifics later," Recker said. "For now, I just wanna know that you're willing to play ball."

Jerome looked around and started nodding his head. "Yeah. Yeah, I'm on the team. As long as I don't have to go deep undercover or nothing. Playing secret agent ain't for me."

"All we'll want you to do is make a couple phone calls, maybe meet with him again, the same way you did before. Nothing different."

"All right then, yeah, yeah, you can count me in."

"Good. We'll be in touch."

"When?"

"Probably tomorrow," Recker replied. "Maybe the next day. You'll hear from us."

Recker and Haley then turned around and started

walking away, Jerome watching them as they left. "Yeah, that's what I'm afraid of."

Once Recker and Haley got back to the car, they started talking about their plans.

"OK, so we got him on board," Haley said. "Now what?"

Recker turned the engine on and started driving. "I dunno. This is your plan, remember?"

"That doesn't mean I have to do all the thinking."

"Whatever we do, whatever we come up with, has to be compelling enough to get Nowak's crew off their duff to check it out. And whatever it is, has to be something we can stick with for a few days in case they don't check it out at first, or they just do a scouting mission to make sure it's legit."

"What would be big enough to make them check it out?" Haley asked, more talking out loud to himself and thinking than actually wanting an answer.

"Our office," Recker said.

"What?"

"What's bigger than our office and where we work out of? Our base of operations. Who wouldn't want to know that?"

"We can't give that up."

"I'm not saying we give up our actual office. We find some place that we can use as a dummy, put some desks and computers in there, make it look legit."

Haley got a grin on his face, liking the idea, thinking it could work. They drove back to the office to talk to Jones about it and get his input. Though he was initially unsure of the plan, Recker and Haley eventually started to sway him to their line of thinking.

"Even if we do this," Jones said. "We'd have to rent or buy something in a very short amount of time and that will positively raise red flags in their book."

"Could you do some of your computer mumbo-jumbo to change the records and sale dates and things like that?" Recker asked.

"Perhaps, but then I also have to change real estate listings and any website that has ever mentioned the property and make sure the dates align."

"But you could do that, right?"

"Yes. In theory, I could. Yes."

"So, there you go."

"Even if I were to agree with this plan, there are some things worth mentioning."

"Always are," Recker said.

"First off, even if this works and draws them to this fake building of ours, Nowak herself is unlikely to attend any festivities. In fact, I downright guarantee it."

"So do I."

"Well then what's the point?"

"The point is to get them back on their heels. They've been dishing things out for a while now. It's time for them to take it."

"Even besides that," Haley said, jumping into the conversation. "Anything involving us, they're going to send their best people. I mean their absolute best. That means Milton, and Jackson, and Martinez, and whoever else they got at the top of their list. She's not sending Joe Schmoe and the rest of the slobs to take us out. She's sending her best."

"He's right," Recker said. "And if we can take out her top tier, that gives us a significant advantage and puts her on the defensive. She's gonna have to be a lot more careful from here on out if she doesn't have her best guys anymore."

"Fine," Jones said. "Even if I agree to all that and say you guys are correct, which you probably are, there's still the rather tall task of identifying a place to set this trap of yours. That's not exactly going to be easy."

"No, you're right. It's got to be a perfect spot. And preferably away from people in case things get out of hand quickly."

"And that will take more time to find something than you probably want it to."

Recker threw his hands up. "What else can we do? It takes what it takes."

Haley then tapped Recker on the arm a couple times with the back of his hand. "What if it doesn't?"

"Huh? Wanna explain that?"

"Vincent."

"What about him?"

"Didn't he say the next time we do something we should do it together?"

"Yeah."

"Well this is it," Haley said. "Think about it. Vincent's already got control of dozens, if not hundreds of proper-ties all over the city. He might already have something we can use. We can get set up quickly."

"But Nowak's been hitting his properties over the past few weeks and months," Jones said.

"I'm sure she doesn't know them all. I would bet Vincent's got some that aren't well known."

Jones looked to Recker for a response. "Yeah, that might work," Recker said.

"Would he agree to it?" Jones asked.

"If he really wants to get rid of her, he will."

"What do you think?" Haley asked.

"Let's give it a try," Recker replied.

Recker immediately called Vincent and requested a meeting. He couldn't get through to the crime lord, but tried his right-hand man, Jimmy, and he set something up for the following morning.

"If he agrees to this," Jones said. "What would be the ideal spot?"

"Preferably something off the beaten path," Recker answered. "A long winding road down a wooded area would be nice. Something fenced and gated, or something that makes them go through a certain area, that way we wouldn't have to guard against multiple entrance points. That reminds me, whatever we get, might be a good idea if you could set up a bunch of cameras, that way we can see what we're dealing with."

"You mean on the perimeter?"

"Yeah. And concealed. That way we could see how many men they're bringing."

"Actually, what I could do is set up main cameras, in plain view, assuming they would take those out, but still having concealed ones. Not having anything visible would be a warning sign to them that something is fishy."

"Good idea."

"Let's just hope that Vincent actually has something in mind," Haley said.

"Oh, he has something," Recker said.

"How can you be so sure?" Jones asked.

"Because it's Vincent. If there's one thing you can always count on him for… it's to be prepared for just about anything. And you know he's got something up his sleeve for a situation like this. You just know it."

**21**

The following morning, Recker and Haley forewent their morning trip to the office, instead heading straight to the diner for their meeting with Vincent. Considering everything that was at stake, and the fact they were going to have to work together anyway, Haley was joining Recker for the meeting this time. Plus, they'd all seen Haley before anyway, so it wasn't like they were revealing a new face. It just didn't matter at this point in trying to conceal him.

They were about ten minutes ahead of schedule for their nine o'clock meeting. Vincent and his crew were already there, like they usually were. Recker and Haley got out of the car and started walking towards the diner.

"No matter how early you get here, you can always count on Vincent getting here first," Recker said. "I think I've only ever beaten him here one time before."

"Maybe he really likes the eggs."

Both men got a chuckle out of it as they reached the door, the burly man in front stopping them. Recker was surprised since he usually had a free pass by now.

"You're good," the man said, looking at Recker. "He's a no-go."

"He's with me," Recker said.

"Orders are orders, man. Just doing what I'm told."

Just then, the front glass door to the restaurant swung open, Malloy standing there. He'd been watching the men approach and saw that Haley got denied entrance.

"It's all right," Malloy said. "Let them both through, it's OK."

The guard stepped aside, letting Haley in as well. He was always under orders not to let anyone else come in besides Recker. Haley by now was in the same graces, but considering he never came to these meetings, he was never really in the thought process for getting a pass. As the two silencers stepped inside, Malloy smiled and greeted each of them with a handshake. He then looked at Haley, surprised to see him.

"Hey, what are you doing out in the daytime?" Malloy said. "I thought sunlight was supposed to kill guys like you?"

Haley chuckled, putting his hand on his chest. "Thought I felt a sharp pain there."

"Seriously though, it's kind of a shock to see you here."

"I thought I'd include him today," Recker said. "You know, kind of like my succession plan. That way if I ever get killed, he'll know the routine."

"What are you talking about?" Malloy asked. "You've

moved into legendary status. Legends never die. They move on sometimes, but they never die."

Recker laughed. "Yeah, I guess we'll see about that one."

Recker and Haley went down to the table where Vincent was sitting. He was already eating as the two men sat down across from him. He put his fork down, stunned to see Haley's presence.

"May I interest you in something?" Vincent asked.

"Nothing for me, thanks," Recker said.

"Yeah, I'll have something," Haley said, not getting the memo that he wasn't supposed to eat.

He drew a look from both men, both of whom were surprised that he was ordering something. Vincent smiled at Haley as he looked at the menu before glancing at Recker.

"You must not have informed him of your usual routine," Vincent said.

"I'll have to work on it next time," Recker replied.

"What?" Haley asked, looking at both men. "I'm hungry. I didn't have breakfast this morning."

Recker let out a laugh, looking down at the table and rubbing the back of his neck.

"You can tell he must be a single man," Vincent said, a waitress coming over and taking Haley's order.

"Do you have a stake in this place?" Recker asked.

Vincent smiled, amused by the question. "No, I do not."

"Oh. Just wondering."

"I assume by the question that you're referring to an ownership interest?"

"What else would there be?" Recker asked with a smile.

"Extortion, protection," Haley said, blurting it right out without a care.

"What do you think?" Vincent asked.

"You already said you didn't," Recker said. "I believe you. I was just asking the question."

"You think I would engage in a protection racket?"

"Why not?" Haley asked. "You wouldn't be the first."

Vincent waved him off, though he wasn't offended or upset by the questioning. "That's a sucker's game. Especially at a restaurant."

"Why?" Recker asked.

Vincent laughed. "Because you never make enemies of the people who prepare your food. They have access to the poison."

Recker and Haley laughed as well, joining their host in his amusement.

"What, you think I have to have a personal interest in a place to eat there?" Vincent asked.

"No, just wondering why you always pick this place for breakfast," Recker replied.

"It has good food," Vincent said, putting a forkful in his mouth. "You would know if you ever joined me in eating."

"I've joined you a few times."

"I believe those times have been well in the past."

"Cheaper to eat in," Recker said.

"Well, I can't really argue there. Probably a more pleasant environment as well," Vincent said, referring to Recker's better half.

"I won't argue there either."

"So, what brings the honor of your partner's presence this morning?"

Recker shrugged. "I don't know. Didn't have anything else to do?"

"Slow day?"

"I dunno. You've met him before. You already know who he is. Guess there really wasn't any point in trying to hide it or pretend he doesn't exist."

"Yeah, I walk, talk, and everything," Haley said, making a joke of it.

They continued small-talking for a little while, at least until Haley's food came. Once he started eating, they got down to business.

"So, what brings us here today?" Vincent asked.

"Nowak," Recker answered.

"I kind of assumed as much."

"We think we might have a plan to stop her. Or at least pay her back for some of the nonsense she's put us all through lately. And you did mention that we should work together the next time either of us got anything."

"I'm all ears."

Recker then told Vincent the plan they'd come up with so far, hoping that he'd have something to add. Vincent kept quiet as Recker explained everything, but by the continuous nodding of his head, it seemed to Recker and Haley like he was on board with it. After he'd said everything, Recker turned it over to Vincent for his opinion.

"Well that's it in a nutshell," Recker said. "What do you think?"

"I think it has a lot of promise. I do question whether it will actually lead to our end goal of eliminating Nowak though."

"It's unlikely that she'd actually be there, much like you wouldn't be there if the tables were reversed. But it could be a serious shot across her bow."

Vincent rubbed his hands together, processing it some more. "There's no doubt about that."

"Think of how disorganized you would be if Malloy and three or four more of your top guys were taken out," Haley said. "Even if it doesn't lead to her directly, she's gonna have some serious reorganizing to do."

"And I think it's either going to make her crawl back into the woodwork or it'll make her more vulnerable," Recker said. "Because if she loses a bunch of her top guys, her best guys, her most loyal guys, she's either going to have to promote from within and risk guys not able to do the job, or she's going to have to go recruiting. Either way, it's going to put her behind the eight-ball."

Vincent put his index finger on his cheek and the others on his lip, with his thumb resting underneath his chin, looking past his two guests as he thought about their plan. Recker and Haley looked at each other as Vincent deliberated. Though it would have been nice if Vincent threw his weight behind the plan, it wouldn't have changed anything for them. They were still going to go through with it whether Vincent got behind it or not. It may have been a bit more difficult, and perhaps taken a little longer, but Recker and Haley were going to embark on it regardless of Vincent's decision.

After thinking for a minute or two, Vincent took his hand off his face and put it on the table. "What do you need from me?"

"Does that mean you're in?" Recker asked.

"Let's just say that I am."

"We would need a place to lure them in. It's gonna take more time for us to set that up ourselves. If you already have a place we can use, that would be more ideal. It's gonna have to be something that's private. A place they don't know about yet. If they know it's owned by you it's gonna be a tough sell. They'd probably think it's a setup or something. Preferably, it would be something we're able to draw them in, then contain them without them being able to escape."

"You have a place like that?" Haley asked.

Vincent nodded, not taking long to answer. "Yes, I do."

"You OK with it getting shot to pieces?" Recker asked.

"I'm not worried about that. What else would you need?"

Recker looked at Haley, before turning back to Vincent. "Men. As many of your boys as you can spare."

"You've got them. As many as you want."

"And Malloy. I don't wanna be giving your men orders."

"They'll take orders from whoever I tell them to."

"I don't doubt that," Recker said. "I would just prefer

not to be bossing around men that don't work for me. I'll work with Malloy and he can tell them what to do from there."

"Done. What kind of time frame are we looking at here?"

"Well, as soon as you give us access to the spot, we can start setting up. So, the sooner the better."

"You can get in as soon as today if you want."

"That'll work," Recker replied. "We need to make it look like an actual office, like something we're actually working out of."

"I'll have some of my men start clearing things out for you as soon as we're done here."

"Good. Then it might take a day or two to get word to Nowak from our informant we got lined up. So, with any luck, we'll be able to start knocking some heads around within a few days."

Vincent smiled, liking the plan better the more he thought about it. "Excellent. Let the bloodletting commence."

## 22

R ecker, Jones, and Haley arrived at the property Vincent owned off of State Road, near the Pennypack Creek and the county prison. It didn't look like much, but then again, it wasn't supposed to. It had been used mostly as a trailer storage facility for semi's, though it hadn't really been active for over a year, which was right around the time Vincent purchased the place. He had plans to renovate the property, but with other matters taking up most of his time since then, he never really got around to it.

For Recker and the team, though, it pretty much suited their needs perfectly. There was a little office on the corner of the property, with close to fifty trailers in front of and next to it, almost making the small building invisible from the street. The entire property was fenced with a ten-foot-high wired fence along with two gates, one for the entrance, and one for the exit. Once they got

Nowak's men into the property, they should be able to trap them there.

Once Recker and company arrived at the trucking facility, both gates were already open, in anticipation of their arrival. They drove right in, stopping in front of the office building. Though nobody was outside to greet them, the team got out of their car and started walking around the property to inspect it.

"What do you think?" Jones asked.

Recker looked around, sizing everything up in his mind. "I think it'll work. Chris?"

"Yeah, looks good to me," Haley replied.

"All these trailers around here could have an adverse effect on our efforts," Jones said. "We wanted to be the ones hidden, but it could create the opposite effect on our intentions and hide them as well."

"I think it'll be fine," Recker said. "Remember, we can move these things around however we need to and put them where we want."

"That's true."

They continued discussing their options for the next few minutes, trying to figure out where they wanted Nowak's men to enter. Malloy came out of the office area, heading straight for them as they talked by the trailers. He shook hands with each of them, interjecting himself into the conversation.

"We were just talking about these trailers," Jones said. "You have a truck that can move these if we want?"

"Absolutely," Malloy answered. "Consider it a blank canvas. Whatever you want, we can do it."

"We were trying to figure out where they're likeliest to come in at," Recker said.

Malloy then pointed to the fence, drawing attention to the wires on top of it. "Well, considering it's got two strands of barbed wire, and it's electrified on top, I doubt they're coming over it."

"No, they'd either snip through the fence somewhere or just break open the gate."

"They wouldn't do that the first time they're here though," Haley said. "They'll observe from a distance to make sure we're really here. They wouldn't risk cutting through the fence until they're ready to strike."

"Yeah, if they cut the fence to get a closer look, and we found it, they'd have to think we'd fly the coop before they're able to get back again with a bigger team to take us out."

"We'll need cameras along the entire perimeter," Jones said. "Or at least something that gives us a wide view of it."

"And don't forget, some have to be visible or they'll know something's up."

"No worries there."

"Come take a look at the office," Malloy said. "See if that works for you."

"As long as it's got four walls it should work for us," Recker said. "We don't really plan to spend much time in it. The rest of the property's the bigger deal."

"Well, let's take a look at it, anyway."

They followed Malloy to the office area, finding it completely empty. Malloy and his team had spent the last couple of hours removing whatever furniture, boxes, and items had been left there from the last owners.

"What do you think?" Malloy asked. "This work for you?"

The team looked around, with Jones finally speaking up after a minute. "Yes, this will do. We don't really need to do much. Just put in a couple desks, some computers, monitors, a few cork and dry erase boards, maybe some newspaper clippings, just to make it seem like it's being heavily used. I don't know whether they'll actually check out the office or just stay outside the gate, but if they do find a way in, we need to make it believable."

"We can take care of that."

"Excellent. Are all those trailers outside empty?"

"Most of them, why?"

"Because we could use one of them to set up in," Jones answered. "The office can be a dummy space. I can put a couple computers in the trailer and monitor the cameras that I put up so we can see our friends enter the premises."

"Yeah, whatever one you want."

"Good. How long will it take you to set up the office?"

"Should only take a couple hours," Malloy replied.

"Good. While you're doing that, I can be setting up the cameras."

"How many will you need?" Recker asked.

"Oh, let's say about twelve," Jones said. "I'll use four for dummies, two on the outside of the office, and one on each gate. Then the other eight I'll conceal in various places along the fence, as well as on the office, that way we'll know where they are at all times."

"We have enough?"

"No, I'm going to have to get more."

"You want me to grab them?" Haley asked.

"No, I'll do that myself," Jones answered. "I know what I'm looking for."

The four of them stood around, continuing to talk about the plan for the next few minutes, making sure everyone knew what was going on.

"OK, while you guys are busy with the office and the cameras, I guess we'll start planting the seeds," Recker said. "Should we make it for tonight?"

"I would set it for tomorrow," Jones replied. "I still have to get the cameras, then install them. That might take me most of the day to get everything the way I want them. Plus, I have to test them and get equipment inside the trailer and make sure everything is working properly."

"OK. Tomorrow then."

While Recker really wanted to get things started as soon as possible, he had to fight the temptation to call Jerome. They spent the rest of the day helping Jones get everything he wanted and needed, while Malloy and his men took care of the office area. By the end of the night, they had everything set up just the way they wanted. The office looked like it was actually in use, one of the trailers near the front gate was used as an area for Jones to monitor the cameras, and they determined where everyone would be stationed. If Nowak's men came in, they certainly would never come out.

The following day, with the plan ready to be put into action, before Recker called Jerome, they stationed Haley at the trucking facility. They wanted him to remain there the entire day so he could observe any activity in case Nowak's men got there sooner than they anticipated. They figured Nowak wouldn't get there until well after dark, but just in case she threw a curveball, Haley would be watching the monitors from inside the trailer that Jones had set up. It was about six o'clock when Recker finally called Jerome, waiting until just after the sun went down.

"Hey, it's Recker."

"Oh, hey, what's up?" Jerome said.

Recker thought he picked up some noises and voices in the background. "You someplace you can talk?"

"Uh, yeah, gimme a minute." Jerome was at a local bar, hamming it up with some of his friends. He stepped outside and away from a few people smoking, going around the side of the building. "OK, I'm good."

"You sure?"

"Yeah. I was just having a few drinks. I'm good now."

"OK. It's on. I want you to call your contact."

"What do you want me to say?"

"I want you to tell them that you got a lead from one of your contacts about the location of our office. I'll give you the address."

"That's it?" Jerome asked.

"That's it. I want you to make it sound big, like you got something really huge, ask for a lot of money for the info."

"No sweat, man, I'll just make it sound like I usually do."

"No, it's possible that they won't believe you," Recker said. "If that's the case, I want you to tell them you actually checked it out last night and saw it for your own eyes, that you saw me going into this place."

Recker then gave him the address, which Jerome wrote down on the back of a napkin he had in his pocket. "And what if they just balk at everything? What if they say they don't care or don't want it?"

"Then tell them you'll just flush the address down the toilet and forget about it. Believe me, they'll go for it."

"All right, I can do that. When you want me to do all this?"

"Preferably within the next hour. And call me back to let me know when you do and what they say."

"OK, will do."

"Think you can manage this?"

"Please, man, you know how long I been working the streets? Pfft, like taking candy from a baby."

"That's what I like to hear."

Jerome didn't waste any time in calling Nowak's men. As soon as he hung up with Recker, he called Milton's number, who picked up after two rings.

"Hey…"

Jerome couldn't even get two words out before being admonished. "What are you doing calling this number? I told you never to call me again. Our business is finished."

"Yeah, well, I got something really big I thought you might wanna know about. I mean, this is really big."

Hearing the excitement in his voice, suddenly Milton wasn't so irritated about the call. "Oh yeah? How big?"

"It's huge, man, but if you're not interested..."

"Wait, wait, wait. Just tell me what you got, and I'll let you know if I'm interested."

"Well, first off I heard about what happened at that jewelry store the other night," Jerome said, trying to set things up for him. "Figured you were trying to get The Silencer and maybe things didn't go the way you wanted to."

"You got something for me or not?"

"Maybe. It'll cost you though. Fifty large."

Milton couldn't contain his laughter. "Fifty gees? Are you f'n kidding me?"

"It's big."

"Yeah, well, for fifty gees you better be offering something up on a silver platter for me."

"Maybe I am."

"Just spit it out," Milton said, tiring of the small talk, especially since he didn't want to be talking to him to begin with. "I got things to do here."

"All right, man, all right, cool your jets. One of my informants on the street said he got a line on where The Silencer and his team is setting up shop."

Milton hardly knew what to say at such stunning news. If true, this really was a big find.

"You think that would be worth fifty large?" Jerome asked.

"OK, maybe. Maybe we got something to talk about here. For that type of money, I'm gonna have to run it by a few people."

"All right, that's fine. When you think you might know?"

"Give me an hour. How reliable do you think this information is?"

"Oh, it's legit, my man, it's legit. I actually verified it myself before calling you because I knew you were gonna ask."

"You really know where they're at?" Milton asked.

"Yep. Spot in the northeast. I staked the place out myself last night. Saw The Silencer himself going into the place."

"How do you know it was his place? Maybe he was just visiting somebody. Or maybe he was working on something? Just because he was there doesn't mean anything."

"I dunno, man, I sat there for close to three hours. I saw him unlock a front gate, then go in. Then an hour later I saw his partner do the same thing. Then two hours later I saw the both of them leave together. They weren't in no hurry, I didn't hear any gunshots, they looked as cool and calm as could be. Seemed to me like they belonged there."

"OK, OK," Milton said. "Let me run it up the flagpole and I'll get back to you."

Jerome waited about twenty minutes and was just about to call Recker to let him know he was just waiting on an answer, when Milton called back.

"Yeah?"

"All right, it's a deal," Milton said. "I can only go up to twenty gees though. That's our best offer."

"All right, man, I'll take it. When will I get my money?"

"We gotta check it out first. If it's legit, and they're setting up shop there, then I'll make sure you get your dough. If we go there and it's empty, and it doesn't look like they've been there, or maybe they were just whistling Dixie, then I'm not giving you jack."

"All right, all right, I feel ya."

"We'll go check it out and I'll let you know."

"Within the next few days. I'll get back to you."

Before getting off the phone, Jerome spilled the address that Recker told him to say. A smile came over his face, knowing that he did good. He then called Recker back to let him know everything was good.

"How you making out?" Recker asked.

"It's all good, man. Everything's a go."

"You talked to Milton?"

"Yeah."

"He fall for it?"

"Man, he fell for it hook, line, and sinker," Jerome emphatically said.

"What'd he say?"

"Well, at first he wasn't too pleased to be hearing from me, but when I told him I knew where your base was, he was all ears."

"Just like I figured," Recker said.

"Yeah, so, then I told him I'd let him know for fifty large, and he said he had to ask somebody if he could swing it."

"Probably his boss."

"So, then he called me back and said they could only do twenty, so I took it."

"He say when he was coming?"

"Nah, didn't say. I tried to pin him down, but he wasn't too talkative, and I didn't wanna press him and give the jig up."

"No, you did right," Recker said.

"He said they'd check it out in the next few days and get back to me. Said they'd only pay if it turned out to be legit."

"Oh, they'll pay. They'll pay in spades."

"You know, I just got to thinking."

"Try not to do too much of that," Recker joked.

"Nah, I'm serious."

"What?"

"I just realized that once they go there and realize that they've been played, they might come back after me, thinking I pulled a fast one on them."

"I wouldn't worry too much about that."

"Why not?"

"Because after we're through with them, there won't be any of them left to come after you."

**23**

After getting off the phone with Jerome, Recker immediately called Jones and Haley to let them know Nowak's crew was coming. He knew Nowak wouldn't be waiting. They'd be coming tonight. Jones and Haley were waiting inside one of the trailers, monitoring the cameras they placed along the perimeter. Recker also let Malloy know, who had men placed in various spots on the property. A few were waiting inside the office. A few were placed along the outside of the fences in all directions. And a few were waiting in vacant trailers, lying down on their stomachs, as the doors were open just enough to see anyone walking by them. They were all ready and prepared for anything to come their way.

For his part, Recker had to wait. He had to wait until Haley gave him the word that Nowak's men were watching the property. Nowak's boys most likely weren't going to enter until they had visual proof that Recker and the team were actually and actively using the property. So Recker was waiting further down the street until they knew for sure that Nowak's bunch were out there.

They weren't sure how long it would take. If Nowak's bunch just wanted to do a quick look to see if it was legit, it probably wouldn't take long. It would probably be just a couple of guys waiting across the street in a car and watching. But if they had something else in mind, something with a little more action, then it might take a while for Nowak's clan to get organized and get enough manpower. Either way was fine for Recker. He probably would have preferred them to just bring down the whole organization and get into a battle royal and fight until the last man was standing. He hated the whole cloak and dagger charade that Nowak was playing, mostly because it took his attention off of what should have been their main focus, and that was helping innocent people who truly needed help.

It took a few hours, but eventually, it looked like they were ready to get things started. A little after nine o'clock, a car drove by, but instead of continuing going down the street, pulled into the parking lot of a manufacturing business located across the street. Jones and Haley were watching on a monitor, observing them parking the car and turning off their lights. There were no other movements after that.

"That's gotta be them," Haley said.

"Yes, but we didn't get a good shot of the license plate or the occupants inside," Jones replied.

"That business they're sitting in front of has been

closed for four hours. No reason for anybody to just be sitting there."

"Unless of course it's a young couple satisfying some urges." Haley just looked at his partner, surprised that he would suggest such a thing. "Or maybe it's a couple of teenagers getting high."

"Should we have Mike drive by and see if the windows are foggy?"

Jones grinned. "It might not be such a bad idea."

Haley then called Recker to let him know what they had and to get his opinion. "Hey, we picked up something."

"What?"

"A car pulled up and parked across the street. They're just sitting there with their lights off."

"Nowak?"

"Ahh, it's tough to say. I assumed it was, but David pointed out it could be some people making out, or a couple of kids blowing their minds."

"That would be a big coincidence," Recker said. "Those things happening on the same night we set some-thing up."

"Yeah it would."

"That's why I don't buy it. It's them. It's gotta be."

"What do you wanna do?"

"Let's go under the assumption it's them. If it's not, no real harm done."

"True."

"How long they been sitting there?" Recker asked.

"About five minutes now."

"Let's give it another twenty minutes. If it's those other things they'll be gone by then."

"Sounds good."

"And if it's Nowak's bunch, if they're just scouting, then they'll either leave as soon as I show up, or they'll wait and leave right after I do and try to tail me."

"Yeah, probably right about that."

For the next twenty minutes, they waited. There was still no movement from the car. They couldn't quite tell what was happening inside the car, but nobody was getting in or out, and the lights remained off, so whoever it was seemed like they were staying for a while. Haley then contacted Recker again to let him know.

"Still sitting there."

"All right, I'm gonna make my way in," Recker said. "Did you let Malloy know to be on the lookout?"

"Yeah, him and his boys are ready."

"OK. Coming in."

"On his way," Haley said to Jones, picking up his pistol and rifle to make sure they were loaded, anticipating a fracas breaking out.

It was only a two- or three-minute drive to the trucking facility from Recker's spot, so he was there in no time. He parked just in front of the entrance gate, the headlights of his car shining brightly upon the gate as he got out to unlock the padlock. As he got out, and back into the vehicle, he made sure he didn't make any eye contact with the car across the street, pretending like it wasn't even there. With the gate now open again, he drove into the property, then got out of his car again to close the gate.

"Well, he's selling it as well as he can," Haley said, looking at the monitor.

Recker drove up to the office area and went inside, turning the lights on. He stayed for over an hour, just sitting there, waiting for word from Haley on what was going on outside.

"The car move yet?" Recker asked.

"Not a peep."

"They're waiting on me for sure."

"Yeah, might be," Haley replied. "When you figuring on leaving?"

"I dunno. Maybe give it another hour, just to keep everything on the up-and-up. Let me know if they move."

"Will do."

Another hour passed by, and the car across the street still didn't move from its spot. As they waited, another thought came into Haley's head.

"You know, all this time we're thinking it might be Nowak, but what if it's the cops? What if they followed Malloy and his bunch here and are wondering what we're doing? And now they've seen Mike."

"Oh, please don't even suggest such a thing," Jones said, shuddering the thought. "Let's not even think about that possibility. I already have enough bad thoughts running through my head without adding to them."

"All right, I'm heading out," Recker said. "It's been two hours. That's plenty of time. They're obviously not coming in. And there's nobody else out there, right?"

"Nope, just the one car is all we see."

"OK. Let's see what happens when I leave. That oughta trigger something."

"Damn well better."

Recker left the office and got back in his car, driving toward the exit gate. Once again, he got out to unlock it, then drove through the opened gate. Then he got out of his car to close it up again, making sure it was locked. He still made sure he didn't make eye contact with the car across the street. Recker drove away, and not even a minute after he left, the car across the street turned its lights on, then pulled out of the parking lot.

"We might be up," Haley hopefully said.

The car drove across the street, stopping just in front of the trucking facility entrance gate. The passenger door opened up and a man got out.

"Who is that?" Haley asked, not yet getting a good view of the man through the cameras.

Once the man got to the gate, he checked on the padlock, then took a closer look at the rest of the fence, walking the length of it as he inspected it.

Jones and Haley looked at each other with a sense of satisfaction once the man's face became clearer.

"Mr. Milton," Jones said.

A wide smile came over Haley's face, pleased with the results. "Looks like we hit pay dirt."

After a few minutes inspecting the fence and looking through it at the rest of the property, Milton got back in his car, then drove away. They immediately contacted Recker to let him know.

"Hey, is that car still there?" Recker asked. "Because I haven't seen it following me."

"No, it just left," Haley replied. "I think you can turn around now, we got what we were looking for."

"How's that?"

"After you left, the car drove up to the fence and started looking it over."

"You get a good look at him?"

"Oh yeah. It's Milton."

Recker grinned, also satisfied with how the plan was shaping up so far.

"You think they'll be back tonight?" Haley asked.

"I dunno. Let's be ready if they are. I'll come back now in case they do."

"How long you wanna wait?"

"All night. If they don't strike tonight, I imagine they'll do it tomorrow."

"Let's hope they don't drag this out."

"No chance of that," Recker said. "They won't wanna risk us getting jumpy and packing up and moving. They'll strike. Either tonight or tomorrow."

"They're gonna be in for a big surprise."

"Yeah. Let's just make sure we put a big bow on it."

Recker came back to the facility, joining Jones and Haley in one of the trailers, as Malloy's men readied themselves in various locations, including the office, where they made sure to keep a light on. It was a long wait, though, and one that didn't wind up being productive, as there wasn't another hint of Nowak's men anywhere. They didn't decide to call it a night until three in the morning, giving their opponents every opportunity to hit them. Once they did pack up, they agreed with Malloy to come back to the following day, just before the sun went down, giving them plenty of time to get ready for the action. And they wanted to make sure they got there before Nowak's crew showed up, which they didn't figure would happen until after dark.

"Here's to hoping we have some fireworks tomorrow," Malloy said.

"There will be," Recker replied. "Just a question whether we're getting the big ones or the little firecrackers."

"It'll be the real deal. I can feel it."

"Let's hope you got some good intuition."

**24**

———

It was a long, and impatient wait for everyone involved. All they wanted to do was get this over with. Recker and the team made sure they kept their day clear, not wanting to get mixed up in something that would take all day to rectify the issue. Luckily, nothing major came up, as they wouldn't have been able to turn their backs on a big problem, regardless for what it meant for their plan with Nowak. But if it was something that could wait, it would wait another day.

Everyone got to the trucking facility around five o'clock, making sure they had plenty of time until Nowak's bunch got there. They put every light on in the office building, making sure it could be seen that someone was in there. That's where they were hoping Nowak's team would go once they got through the gate. Jones got in his spot in the trailer, looking at the cameras, while Recker and Haley took up other spots to be more readily available when the action hit. While they were figuring out their respective spots, Haley noticed the vest Recker was wearing, which he seemed to be doing more frequently lately.

Haley tapped the vest. "Is this like your AMEX card now? Can't leave home without it."

"Doesn't hurt to be prepared. Especially since it's saved my life already."

"I hear ya. I'm not poking fun, I should probably start wearing one myself."

"Probably would be a good idea. Especially when you're around me. I seem to have a black cloud over me."

"I don't think that cancels out the angel on your shoulder."

"Huh?"

"Mia?"

"Oh," Recker said with a laugh. "Yeah."

They then departed, each taking opposite ends of the yard. Recker dropped to the ground to lie underneath a trailer near the front gate, though there were still a couple trailers in front of it, so he would still be concealed by the darkness from anyone entering. Haley went to the back corner, standing between a trailer and the corner of the fence.

It wasn't until after ten that they finally started to see some movement. Everyone, including Malloy and his men, had an earpiece that was linked up with Jones, so he could inform everyone at the same time what he was seeing on the cameras.

"Several cars just drove by and parked across the street," Jones said.

"Is that for us?" Recker asked.

"I would say so. Looks like they're getting out."

"How many?"

"Five cars," Jones answered. "Four men in each car."

Milton led the charge of the twenty men, but Recker and the team weren't discouraged by the number. They were actually quite satisfied. With the help of Vincent's men, they had more than enough to handle them. Not including Jones, who was fairly useless with a weapon, they had twelve men of their own. And Recker and Haley always counted themselves as being able to take out four or five men on their own, so they were confident it wasn't a problem. If anything, it just took a larger chunk out of Nowak's numbers, crippling her more quickly.

"They're walking across the street," Jones said. "Heading for the gate."

"Not very creative," Recker quipped.

"Wait, a few of them are breaking off and going around the side. Looks like half." Jones counted the men on the screen. "Yes, ten have broken off the main group and are moving around the side."

"Malloy, those are all you," Recker said.

"We got them," Malloy replied.

"They just took out the fake cameras," Jones said. "Now they just broke the chain on the front gate. They're coming in."

"OK," Recker said. "Everybody be ready. This is it."

Milton, leading the group in, instructed some of his men to loop around the trailers, that way they'd come up on the office in three spots, including the men coming around the side, that way they could surround it. The men were also instructed by Milton to look out for signs of a trap. Absent that, they all were to meet up at the office, which they did within a few minutes. Once they reconvened at the office, one of the men snuck up to a window, peering in to see if anyone was inside. He then reported back to Milton.

"Looks like one guy inside," the man inside.

"Was it him?" Milton asked.

"His back is turned, but it looks like him. Same haircut, same build."

"It's gotta be him. All right, let's do this. You guys got the window. We'll take the door."

Just as they were about to shoot, gunfire erupted from the roof of the building. Some of Malloy's men looked down and started picking some of Nowak's men off. As Milton and company returned fire, more of Vincent's men threw open a trailer door, ripping off shots themselves. Not wanting to stand out in the open and get caught in the crossfire, Milton and a few others burst through the office door, only to see five more of Vincent's men waiting for them, unleashing a barrage of gunfire.

Milton and the rest of his group were now dead, but the rest of the bunch that were on the side had now made their way inside, cutting through the fence with bolt cutters. Recker and Haley came out from their spots and joined the action, cutting down the rest of Nowak's men with ease. It was a furious and intense battle, but it was short-lived, and lasted less than five minutes from when the first shots were fired.

After it was over, Recker and Haley looked at each other, thinking that was actually easier than they expected. They thought there'd at least be a little bit more of a fight. As it was, neither of them hardly broke a sweat. Malloy's team did most of the heavy lifting, which was fine by Recker. It was about time they had an easy time of it, he thought.

"David, anything else going on out there?" Recker asked, wanting to make sure there wasn't a second wave coming.

"Everything is clear."

"Keep a lookout while we clean up back here."

"I will, but if I may make a suggestion, I would suggest that you hurry up. Somebody surely heard the barrage of gunfire and I would think the police would be here soon."

"Be out in less than five."

"OK," Jones nervously said.

Recker and Haley walked over some of the fallen bodies, making their way to Malloy, who was standing near the door of the office. Malloy had a satisfying smile on his face, pleased with how everything turned out.

"About time we turned the tables on these schmucks," Malloy said.

"How'd you guys make out?" Recker asked. "Any of your boys hurt?"

"Two guys, nothing major though, they'll survive."

"One of them's still alive down here," one of Malloy's men said.

"Finish him," Malloy replied.

"No, wait," Recker said, thinking the injured man

might still be of some use to them. "He might know something about Nowak."

The three of them went down to the location of the nearly dead man, lying by one of the windows of the building. Recker knelt next to the man, who looked like he was losing a large amount of blood from his midsection. Recker felt badly for him, thinking he wasn't much more than twenty years old, if he was even that.

"You're hurt bad, son," Recker said, grabbing the kid's hand.

The man took a second to reply, finding it hard to get the energy to speak. "I know."

"I'll tell you what I can do. If you tell me where Nowak is right now, I'll call for an ambulance to take you to the hospital. It's the only chance you've got."

The man looked at him, almost not believing him. "You would do that?"

"Nothing here's personal. At least not with you. I don't have any desire to see you dead. But you gotta decide now before it's too late."

The man slightly nodded his head. It was the best he could do. "She lives at 6826 Wilshire Road. She's waiting on a report from us."

"How many men she got there with her?"

"Umm, I dunno, not many. Most were here. Maybe six or eight, something like that."

Recker felt a tap on his shoulder and looked back, seeing Haley's hand on him.

"Sirens," Haley said. "We gotta go."

"I'll round up my boys," Malloy said.

"All right, you just sit tight and hang in there," Recker said, talking to the kid. "Help's on the way, OK?"

The man nodded, not sure if he was going to make it.

Recker looked back to Haley. "Help David clear his equipment out."

As Malloy's bunch rushed to their cars, and Haley ran to the trailer to help Jones empty it, Recker remained stationary, trying to help the kid remain calm in the face of his impending death. About thirty seconds later, the young man closed his eyes for the final time. Though Recker heard the police sirens getting closer, he wasn't in any rush. He finally let go of the kid's hand and gently placed it on his bullet-ridden stomach. Though they were technically on opposite sides, there was something about seeing him dead that made Recker feel a sense of sadness.

Haley and Jones came out of the trailer, each hurrying to their car with laptops under their arms. Haley looked over and saw Recker still standing over the kid.

"Mike, come on!" Haley yelled.

Recker looked over and finally got his feet moving, running over to them.

"We're all done, let's go," Haley said.

The three of them got in their car and took off, speeding out of the property and down the road, only a minute behind Malloy's bunch. As they drove away, they could see the bright lights of the police cars driving onto the trucking facility.

"We heading to Nowak's?" Haley asked, since he was driving.

"Yeah, let's end this," Recker answered. He then

patched himself through to Malloy, letting him know of their plans. "Malloy, we're heading to Nowak's now."

"So are we," Malloy replied. "We're only a minute or two ahead of you. We'll wait for you before we move in."

"Roger that."

It was only a ten-minute drive before they got to Nowak's address, a newly cleared street with homes that were only built in the past six months. Each home was over three thousand square feet, with updated features, costing well over six-hundred thousand dollars. It was a secluded street, with only a couple of homes on it. Nowak's was the last one, with woods on the side of it.

"You know, she might have cleared out by the time we get there," Haley said. "Especially if she's tried to contact her team and they're not answering, she might assume something's up and get out."

"Could be," Recker replied.

Their suspicions were soon answered, as a few minutes before they got there, they heard gunfire.

"Looks like we're already too late," Haley said.

They drove onto her property, already seeing Malloy's team out of their vehicles and engaged with Nowak's men.

"Someone's a little overeager," Jones said.

Seeing several dead men in the driveway already, Recker and Haley jumped out of the car, running over to Malloy's car.

"Sorry," Malloy said. "They came running out of the house, looked like they were about to jet out of here. Had to start without you."

"Probably realized what happened to the others," Recker said.

"Yeah, that's what I figured. I got some of my boys already heading around the back to make sure she doesn't slip out back there."

Malloy then heard the voice of one of his men in his ear. "Nowak started coming out back here but retreated back inside."

Malloy grinned. "We got her trapped."

"Back door's secured. We're going in."

After the last of Nowak's men in the front dropped dead by the front door, Malloy gently tapped Recker on the arm. "Let's get this."

They all ran toward the front door, passing over four of Nowak's men, not one of them still living. They broke through the front door and started clearing each room. With all of the help they had, they quickly cleared the first floor. While some of the men went to the second floor, Recker, Haley, and Malloy went down to the finished basement. About halfway down the steps, they ducked to avoid incoming gunfire. They quickly rushed down the steps, identifying their targets, the last two remaining men that Nowak had.

With Nowak nowhere in sight, they started checking doors. One housed the electrical system, one had plumbing pipes, and one led to what was being used as a games room. Nowak stood there, in front of a pool table, seemingly resigned to her fate. She knew there was no escape, not unless she was somehow able to reason with them.

"I can make you all extremely wealthy," Nowak said. "Work for me and anything you desire is yours."

"I don't do things for money," Recker said.

Nowak shrugged. "Well, I'm unarmed, and I don't plan on putting up a fight. And I don't peg you for a man who would shoot an unarmed woman, so I don't know what you plan on doing here."

Recker sighed. "You're right. I wouldn't shoot an unarmed woman."

Then a shot rang out, Recker quickly snapping his head to look over his shoulder. He saw Malloy, still holding the gun in his hand, pointing at Nowak's direction.

"I don't have the same reservations," Malloy said.

Recker said nothing but turned his head back around to see Nowak's body lying on the floor. Haley went over to it, turning her lifeless body over and seeing the hole in the middle of her forehead. He just looked up at his partner and shook his head, letting him know she was gone. Recker turned around and just looked at Malloy.

"Had to be done," Malloy said. "We both know that."

Recker solemnly nodded, agreeing with him on principle. Haley then walked by the both of them, tapping Recker on the arm.

"C'mon, we gotta get out of here before the cops get here too," Haley said.

The entire team cleared out of the house and was gone within a minute, long before the police were to get there. Once back in their car, Haley started driving away, Jones wondering what happened.

"Should I ask?" Jones said.

"Nowak's dead," Recker replied.

"How?"

"Malloy."

"Should I inquire about the details?"

"Let's not argue about semantics now," Recker said. "She's gone, that's the only thing that matters anymore. She's gone and we don't have to worry about her again."

"I guess that is the main thing, isn't it? Now we can get back to our normal business."

"At least until the next big thing comes along. And as I'm sure we all know by now… something else will come along."

# LETHAL FORCE PREVIEW

Enjoy the following 3 chapter sample of the next book in The Silencer Series, Lethal Force.

**25**

———

Recker left the office to go home, already knowing he was in for a rough night. Mia was taking another nurse's shift, on top of her own, so she was working a double, and wouldn't get done until around seven in the morning. Anytime Mia wasn't there at night, Recker seemed to have a tougher time of it. Not only did he have a harder time getting to sleep without her being next to him, it seemed his dreams were even worse when she wasn't there. Maybe it was just because she had a way of calming him down after he woke up from what seemed like a nightly occurrence and knowing she wouldn't be there this time was stroking his fears even worse than usual.

Recker's fears were rightly founded, as even though he put his head down on a pillow at eleven o'clock, he didn't drift off to sleep until about two. He tossed and turned, unable to turn his mind off from thinking horrible thoughts. And it was another rough one for him once his eyes closed for good. The nightmares started only a few minutes after falling asleep.

*Recker walked into the cafeteria at the hospital, sitting at his usual table as he waited for Mia to come down from the pediatric wing. Almost immediately after sitting down, he saw her beautiful face walk in. Recker stood up and kissed his black-haired beauty once she got to the table.*

*"So, what's this about?" Mia asked. "What's the big emergency that couldn't wait until I got home?"*

*"I just had to call you and let you know."*

*"Know what?"*

*"I think I'm done with it all."*

*"You are?"*

*"Yeah," Recker said. "I'm just done. I'm tired. The constant danger, the injuries, the physical toll, the mental damage, I just can't do it anymore."*

*"Stop. Don't talk like that. You know you don't mean it. It's just the dreams that are doing it to you."*

*"No, I'm really serious. I'm not sure I wanna do this anymore."*

*"It's just the dreams playing tricks with your mind, Mike."*

*"This isn't a dream talking. It's how I really feel. I just wanna rest. For good."*

*"You can't rest. If you rest, you'll die. You need this to keep going."*

*"All I need is you," Recker said. "This is what you've always wanted, isn't it? For me to give it all up?"*

*"What would David and Chris say?"*

"They'll understand. They'll keep going. They'll do what needs to be done."

"It's not that easy, Mike."

"Of course it is. Why wouldn't it be?"

"Because you don't really mean it. It's just the dreams talking."

"Stop saying that. It's not."

"But it is," Mia said. "You know it is. Just listen to yourself. The real you would never talk like that."

"I've changed."

"Men like you don't change so easily."

"I don't understand why you're saying this. I thought you'd be happy."

"Mike, I need you to wake up now."

"What? Why?"

"Because if this dream continues, I'm going to die."

"What? No!"

"You can't stop it, Mike."

Recker immediately started looking around frantically, searching for the first sign of trouble. There was none to be found though.

"I can stop it. I can stop everything."

"You're not superhuman, Mike. You can't save everyone. Not even me."

"Stop talking like that."

"You know why you keep having these dreams, don't you?"

"No, why?"

"Because you're afraid of losing me. You know, deep down inside, that as long as you do what you do, eventually one of us *is going to be ripped away from the other. You know that's true."*

*"No, it's not."*

*Mia put her hand on Recker's face and smiled. "You know it is. Denying it isn't helping you. It's only prolonging your torture."*

*"I'm not going to lose you."*

*"Mike, it's already predetermined. My fate was sealed the moment you walked into my life. There's nothing you can do to prevent it."*

*"I can. I promise you that won't happen."*

*Mia sighed and shook her head, knowing how stubborn he could be. "You keep having these dreams because you know with each passing day, the odds are only increasing that one day, one of us won't be here any longer. We'll never grow old together. That's just not how it works for men like you. You go down in a blaze of glory, not in a nursing home."*

*"That's why I'm quitting."*

*"You'll never quit. It's just not in you. Everything's in your head right now. Your dreams are simply your fears for the future, what you know is likely to be true. You'll probably always have them. They're not going to stop anytime soon."*

*"I promise you that's not how we'll end up. It's not how you'll end up. I won't let that happen."*

*"It's too late, Mike. It's already begun."*

*"What has?"*

*Mia turned her head, looking back to the cafeteria entrance doors. Recker's eyes glanced over to them as well. They saw Haley walking in, followed closely by Jones.*

*Mia turned back to Recker and smiled. "There they are."*

Recker looked confused. "Why are they here? I didn't tell them to come."

"You still don't get it, do you? It's just part of the dream."

As Haley and Jones approached the table, Recker and Mia stood up.

"What are you guys doing here?" Recker asked.

"We're here because of you," Jones replied.

"I don't understand. What's that mean?"

"It means you're done. You really thought you could just walk away from us and not have any consequences?"

"You guys can do the job without me," Recker said.

"Nobody walks away from us."

"Just listen to them, dear," Mia said, putting her hand on her boyfriend's face again.

"It's time to end this," Haley said.

"End what?"

"You need to come back to us without having all these other things to worry about."

Recker looked like he still didn't understand. Mia turned back around to face her friends. Haley pulled a gun and pointed it at her.

"I'm ready," Mia said.

"What?" Recker said. "What's going on?"

"This has to end," Haley said, holding his arm straighter, getting ready to fire.

Recker couldn't believe what was about to happen. "No, wait!"

Haley fired two times, both bullets entering Mia's midsection. Blood rolled down out of the corner of her mouth as she held her stomach. She smiled at Recker.

*"I love you. But this is how it ends for us."*

*Mia slumped down to the ground as Recker looked on in horror. He looked at his friends, who were simply smiling at him, seemingly pleased with their despicable actions. Recker then flopped down to the ground and held Mia in his arms as the last breath of life faded out of her.*

Recker sat up like he'd been shot out of a cannon, breathing as heavy as if he'd just run a marathon. He looked down at Mia's spot beside him and put his hand on her pillow. He then leaned back, letting his head rest against the wall behind him. He closed his eyes for a moment.

"It was just a dream," he whispered.

Recker looked at the clock and saw it was only two-thirty. He reached over to the end table and grabbed his phone. He scrolled down to Mia's number and was about to call her, just wanting to hear her voice for a minute or two, but then put his phone back. If he called for no reason, she was bound to know something was up, and would likely guess at the culprit. He didn't want her worrying about him while she was at the hospital. Instead, Recker slouched back down onto his back, then rolled onto his side as he contemplated whether he even wanted to try to fall back asleep again. At this point, he'd rather be tired than have to relive the same nightmares in his head over and over again.

Eventually, Recker did fall back asleep again, though it took him another hour to do so. He was planning on having breakfast waiting for Mia when she got in since she'd done it for him so many times, not that he planned on anything special, just bacon and eggs, but he was so tired, he slept through his alarm. He did wake up, though, at the sound of keys wiggling and the front door opening. Recker jumped out of bed and went into the living room, him and Mia locking eyes as soon as he appeared in the frame of the door. They both immediately went to each other and embraced, each of them happy to have the other in their arms.

"I was planning on having breakfast ready for you," Recker said. "I overslept a little bit."

"That's sweet of you, thank you."

"Just sit down and I'll make something for you."

"No, that's all right, really... I'm not really hungry."

"Are you sure? It's no trouble."

Mia kissed him on the lips. "Positive. Thank you for the offer, but I'm really just tired more than anything."

"How'd your night go?"

"Long. It was so busy, and we were already short-handed. It felt like everyone in the world had a baby in the last twenty-four hours. How about you? How was your night?"

"Fine."

"Manage all right without me?" Mia asked.

"It was a struggle."

"You look tired."

"I kept waking up. Probably because you weren't next to me."

Mia smiled, though she knew that wasn't the reason. She could guess what his issue was. "You had another one, didn't you?"

"I don't really wanna talk about it. I'm fine."

"Are you sure? It might do you good to get it out of your system."

"No, I'm fine. Really. You're tired anyway. The last thing you need right now is for me to throw some more of my issues on you."

"You know there's nothing else in the world that's more important to me than you are. Tired or not, I'm here."

"I know you are. But I want you to be selfish and take care of yourself for a change. We can always talk about it later."

"OK. What time do you have to leave?"

"Maybe an hour or so."

"You know what I would really like?" Mia asked.

"What's that?"

"For us to just lie down in bed and hold each other until you leave."

Recker smiled at her. "I think we could arrange that."

Recker and Mia went to their bedroom and snuggled each other underneath the sheets. As Recker held her, his mind went back to his dream, seeing her killed right in front of him. He closed his eyes, trying to shut it off, though it was no use. It kept replaying in his mind over and over again. Here he was holding this beautiful woman in his arms, and all he could think about was bad thoughts. He just wanted a positive image entering his mind for a change.

"You guys got anything interesting going on today?"

Mia said groggily, sounding like she was about to drift off to sleep.

"Uh, no, I don't think so. At least nothing I'm aware of. Never know how the day will unfold though."

There was silence for another minute, and though Recker wasn't a big small-talker, he actually preferred it in this instance if it helped to prevent him from what he was previously thinking.

"Hey, if I happen to fall asleep before you go, wake me up before you leave, OK?" Mia said.

"I'm not gonna wake you up. You need to sleep."

"Would you at least kiss me then?"

"There's nothing I would like better." There was silence for another minute. "You think you're gonna sleep the day away?"

There was no reply though. Recker tilted his head away and looked at his girlfriend's face, thinking she looked like an angel when she was sleeping. His thoughts then turned to what Mia said in his dream, about them being one day closer to one of them being ripped away from the other. He hoped this wouldn't be that day.

**26**

———

Recker got to the office, and as often as the case was, Jones and Haley were already there waiting for him. Recker didn't even try to beat them in anymore. It was a useless endeavor. He just wasn't making it there first, or even second on most days. Jones gave Recker a sharp eye when he walked in, then looked at his watch.

"It looks as though you've seen better days already," Jones said. "And it's only nine o'clock."

"You sleep at all?" Haley asked.

"I got a few minutes here and there," Recker answered.

"You've looked tired lately," Jones said. "You're not getting enough sleep."

"I'm fine."

"Perhaps, but, is there something troubling you that's preventing you from sleeping?"

"It's nothing. I'm just having one of those stretches

that everybody gets from time to time when they have trouble falling asleep."

Haley rubbed the stubble on his face, thinking back to a conversation he had with Mia about dreams. He wondered if he should bring it up, knowing he wasn't likely to get the truth anyway, and that it might rub his partner the wrong way. But Haley also thought that if he mentioned it, maybe Recker would know that he knew, and maybe it would be enough to springboard a conversation between the two of them about it. Haley also would have nightmares from time to time, and judging by Recker's appearance lately, and by Mia's conversation, that it was probably worse than anything he'd ever experienced. Haley suspected it was a daily, or at least fairly regular occurrence.

Haley suspected that every operative that had ever been overseas on multiple missions, who'd done some of the things they'd done, would have nightmares sometimes. He just figured it went along with the job. One of the perils of doing the work that they'd done... is that it never really leaves you. Even when it's finished. It always remained in the mind and in the soul. For him, Haley figured he had a bad nightmare about once a month. There didn't seem to be any trigger for it that he could tell. Sometimes it was after a case, sometimes it was in the middle of a dry spell, it didn't seem to matter. He couldn't figure out a cause. It just happened. And as he looked at Recker, there was a man who was carrying around a load with him. He didn't talk about it with Jones, and he wasn't sure if Jones noticed the same things he did, but he could see it on Recker's face, his body language, the way he stood, the way he moved, everything about him. It was a man who seemed tired. Tired of whatever images were flashing around in that head of his.

"Having bad nightmares or anything?" Haley asked, blurting it out.

Jones stopped typing and looked at Recker, wondering if maybe Haley had hit on something.

Recker didn't like being the center of attention and wanted to get this line of questioning over with so they could start their real business. His eyes glanced over between his two friends, without moving his head at all. "No, why?"

"Just asking. Thought maybe that's why you weren't sleeping."

Recker shook his head. "I'm good. Like I said, just one of those stretches. I'm sure I'll get back to normal soon."

"OK," Haley said, not wanting to press him too much on it. Recker was the type of man that the more you dug into him on something, the more he would draw away. That was the last thing anyone needed.

"Now that we're done with the couch and therapy session, maybe we can get back to work now?" Recker asked.

"Excellent idea," Jones said.

"Anything on the agenda?"

"If it happens as I think it will happen, we will probably have a situation come down later today."

"Why? What's up?"

"We picked up some texts and voicemails between

several individuals that I'm putting up on the big screen now."

Recker and Haley walked over to the fifty-inch monitor hanging on the wall, standing inches away from it as Jones started putting his information on it. Pictures of eight men appeared on the screen.

"Pleasant-looking bunch, aren't they?" Haley said.

"Pleasant indeed," Jones replied. "In this case, the looks match the men."

"Bad guys, I take it?" Recker asked.

"Bad doesn't even begin to describe them. This is as rough-and-tumble of a crew as we've ever come across."

Recker shot Jones a look. They'd handled some pretty bad dudes in their time. Saying this group might be the worst was either a bit of a stretch or it would be overly terrifying.

"We've dealt with some pretty bad hombres, David."

"Oh, I'm well aware, believe me. But this crew is a little different than the others we've come across."

"How so?" Haley asked.

"Because they just entirely rely on brute force. Unlike Nowak, Jeremiah, Vincent, or any of the other people we've come across, these guys don't try to outsmart you or make you think they're coming from a different direction. They're coming head on and they don't care if you know it. They're coming straight for you and they dare you to get in their way."

Recker and Haley continued to look at the names and faces on the screen to get familiar with them.

"How come I don't recognize any of these people?" Recker asked.

"Because they've only been here for a few weeks."

"Here? They've moved?"

"Oh, indeed they have," Jones answered.

"Where were they before?" Haley said.

"Mostly New Jersey and Delaware. That's where most of my information is coming from."

"What are they doing here?"

"Establishing a presence."

Recker shook his head as he looked at the screen. "When's it gonna end? Every time a challenger for Vincent's throne gets knocked off, there's a new one coming."

"Well, while I normally would understand the connection, you would be off base in this instance," Jones replied.

"What?"

"This group has no interest in taking over a city from underneath it."

"Then what do they want?"

"The short and easy answer is to take as much money and inflict as much brutality as they can before they move on."

"Why here?" Recker asked. "Why now?"

"As far as I can make out, it is police pressure driving them out. That was the reason they relocated from New Jersey to Delaware initially."

"So, the same thing will happen here."

Jones put his hand up, indicating that would not be as easy as it sounded. "In both cases it took over five years to drive them out. Now if it takes that much time here, then..."

"Then a lot of people are going to get hurt."

"A lot is putting it mildly. The estimates that I could get my hands on indicate that this gang is believed to be responsible for close to a hundred murders in the past ten years. And that's just the start of it. Hundreds of others have been put in the hospital at their hands."

"Who are their usual targets?"

"The best answer I can give you is just about anyone," Jones said. "Young, old, black, white, innocent, criminal, nothing much matters to this bunch. If you've got what they want, they will take it from you. And they will take no prisoners in doing so. They are violent and will use whatever means are at their disposal."

"Is it just these eight?" Haley asked.

Jones didn't immediately reply, causing both men to look back at him. With a sigh, Jones hit a button on his computer, and then looked up at the screen again.

"Hardly," Jones said.

The faces on Recker and Haley pretty much said it all. A look of surprise and horror encapsulated their expressions. They watched as the fairly large pictures of the eight men were replaced with the much smaller pictures of dozens more.

"Is this all of them?" Haley said.

"At least the ones that have been publicly identified," Jones replied. "Who knows how many more they've recruited that aren't known yet?"

"There must be close to a hundred people here," Recker said.

"No, not quite. Only eighty-three."

Recker's eyes almost bulged out of his head as he looked at the screen. "Only eighty-three," he whispered.

"Where are we gonna start?" Haley asked.

"I'm in the process of working on that now," Jones answered.

"They're already here?" Recker asked.

"Indeed, they are."

"For how long?"

"Earliest I can make out is they arrived sometime last week."

"And these are the guys you're saying we might have to deal with today?"

With a worrisome look in his eye, Jones went back to his computer screen. "Unfortunately."

"I'm hoping we're not going to deal with all eighty-three guys today," Recker said.

"I wish I could tell you how many there will be, but I can honestly say that I don't know. It could be three. It could be thirty."

"Wonderful. Just what is it they're going to be hitting today?"

"I'm still working on that," Jones replied.

Recker looked at the time. "Still working on it? When you gonna know?"

"When they say something definitive."

"But you know it's gonna be today?"

"That would be correct. Sometime around three o'clock."

"Well, do you have an area?" Recker asked.

Jones looked up at him. "I do not. I have a time. That's it."

"Just great."

Haley continued looking at the screen, amazed at the amount of people he was watching. "Not that I particularly care about the odds, or being on the short-end of the stick, but how are we gonna go up against eighty-three people?"

"Hopefully one at a time," Jones answered.

"As unlikely as that is," Recker said. "Chris is right. We're gonna need help."

"And just what did you have in mind?"

Recker gave him a grin. "There's only one man in this city that can help."

"Don't say it."

"You know who I'm talking about."

"Why don't we just put our offices next to his?" Jones sarcastically said. "We work with him so much we might as well be paying him rent."

"How organized is this bunch? Do they have a name or anything?"

"Well, they call themselves the Tri-State Scorpions."

Recker wasn't impressed. "Clever."

"As far as being organized, they do not have a de facto leader. They make decisions as a group. Exactly what that process is like or how involved it is I cannot say. It could be something like a general council or it could be everyone."

"So how do they determine what to hit then?"

"As I just explained to you, we don't know. Perhaps there's a ten-person board that approves everything. Perhaps everyone is free to do whatever they like within certain parameters. Perhaps it's some combination of the two. Right now, your guess is as good as mine."

"And how many of them are you tracking right now?"

"Right now, I've got three of their numbers."

"How'd you manage that?" Recker asked.

"Same way I always manage it. The system picked up on a couple of words within the covered radius and alerted me."

"Any idea what they're planning? I know you don't have an address yet, but is it a bank, convenience store, drugstore, anything?"

"Yes. Could be any of the above," Jones replied.

"Thanks. Very helpful."

"I'm giving you all the information I've got at the present time."

"Is it possible this thing could go down without us?"

"Extremely possible."

"Wonderful."

"Stop saying that."

"Is there anything you need us to do?" Recker asked. "Something to speed things along?"

"No, not a thing."

"In that case, I'm gonna make a phone call."

"Don't do it," Jones said.

"Got to."

Jones sighed, already knowing he had lost the battle. Recker was going to call Vincent for help again. He looked up from his computer only to see that Recker was already on the phone.

"Mike, what can I help you with?" Vincent asked.

"It's something urgent. Can we meet today?"

"Uh, yeah, I think I have room in my schedule. How's one o'clock sound?"

"I can make it," Recker said. "Where?"

"Let's make it the same place as usual. I missed breakfast today."

"I'll be there."

As Recker put his phone back in his pocket, he glanced over at Jones, who was sitting at his computer still shaking his head.

"A little more discussion would have been nice before getting us in bed with him again," Jones said.

"We're so far in bed with him at this point, what's the difference? Right now, I'll align myself with anybody to stop what I believe is the greater threat. And right now, it's those creeps on the screen."

## 27

Vincent and Malloy were already sitting down in the conference room of one of their delivery businesses, waiting for their visitors to arrive. The Tri-State Scorpions had already contacted Vincent via a third party to request a meeting, wanting to meet with the crime boss to announce their arrival in the city and surrounding area. Vincent was already well aware of the gang's reputation, and though he'd never formally met them before, both sides knew of the other.

"What did Recker want?" Malloy asked.

"Didn't say. Just said it was urgent."

"Wonder what that's about."

"Don't know," Vincent said. "Could be just about anything."

"What time?"

Vincent looked at his watch. "About two hours from now."

About five minutes later, one of Vincent's subordinates walked into the room to let them know that one of the Scorpions had arrived.

"He been frisked?" Malloy asked.

After getting the word that their visitor was clean, Vincent was eager to have the meeting begin. "Show them in."

"How you think this is gonna go?"

"We shall see."

The door then opened, Vincent's man stepping to the side to let Tommy Billings in. Billings was a fairly big man, standing over six-foot-three, and well over two hundred pounds, and could be an imposing sight with his bald head and goatee. Though Jones was right in that the Scorpions did not have a specific leader, in situations where someone needed to talk for the group, Billings was usually the man for the job. He could be an intimidating figure, he could talk the tough talk when it was needed, but he also was an intelligent guy and didn't succumb to making moves on impulse like many members of the group. While most of the Scorpions did opt for violence and brutality first, and Billings wasn't necessarily opposed to it when necessary, he also knew there were times when a softer touch was needed for the survival of the group. He knew, sometimes, diplomacy was the best option.

Vincent stood up to shake his visitor's hand. "Mr. Billings, pleasure to meet you."

"Likewise," Billings replied, reciprocating the handshake.

Vincent pointed to a chair. "Have a seat."

"Thank you."

Vincent then pointed to his most loyal soldier, seated by his side. "This is Jimmy Malloy."

"Ahh, the famous right-hand man of yours. I've heard of you as well."

"Nothing good I hope," Malloy said.

Billings grinned. "A mixture. Thought you'd be a little taller though."

"Now that the pleasantries are out of the way, what can I do for you?"

"As you may or may not be aware, we've been relocating our base of operations from Jersey the last few years."

"I'm well aware of your migration pattern."

"The heat's been coming down on us pretty good lately."

"And you think it will be easier for you here?"

"Listen, I know you run things around here and you're the top dog, and I totally understand and respect that. We're not looking to get into a war with you. We just want to peacefully coexist together."

Vincent smiled, thinking it was an odd choice of words. "I didn't think peaceful and Scorpions could coexist in the same sentence together."

Billings let out a small laugh. "Fair enough. I should tell you in all honesty, that some of the boys wanted to just roll into town and get rid of whoever gets in our way, you included."

"I should tell you that you wouldn't be the first to try. There were the Italians, Jeremiah, Nowak, and a bunch of other small-timers. I'm still here. They're not."

"We might be a little more formidable than those people."

"Perhaps. Or maybe you would just occupy more space in the cemetery. Make no mistake, I was aware of your presence the minute you drove into town. You see, unlike your crew, war and violence is very seldom my first option or preference. But once I'm there, I will be as ruthless as anyone."

"I don't doubt that."

"You should also know that I operate in many circles. What you see isn't always what you get. And you don't always know where it's coming from."

"I've heard that," Billings said.

"I've got people employed in many different facets. Some work for me directly on a day-to-day basis, some work in financial sectors, some put on a blue suit and patrol around in a police car, some are detectives, some work in various other business interests, and I even have a few working for good old Uncle Sam. Believe me when I tell you, you don't want to make me for an enemy."

Billings nodded, knowing exactly how formidable of a threat Vincent was. Nothing he was hearing was new to him. The rumors of how far Vincent's hand stretched were known far and wide.

"And I believe that. Like I said, I didn't come here to threaten."

"Then what exactly do you want?" Vincent asked.

"Listen, we all know you're a powerful man. You've got

influence all over the place. No one disputes that. I think that if we wanted to take over, we'd have a hell of a fight. We're not some pushovers."

"No question about it."

"You'd have your hands full," Billings said. "Maybe you'd win, but it'd come at a high cost. Just the same, we might win, but it would also come at a high cost."

"Sometimes that's just the price of victory."

"It is. But it's not one we're interested in playing with right now. We're riding in holding the white peace flag so to speak."

"For what purpose?"

"Just for the purpose of coexisting, man. We know us riding in, you could take it as a threat and act out against it. That's not what we want. We also know that if we start hitting places that belong to you, that wouldn't be good either. We just wanna hang around, do our thing, and not have any beef with you."

"So, what, you want my blessing to have you here?"

"If you wanna call it a blessing, sure, I'd prefer to think of it as a truce. Neither side acts out against the other. There's plenty of room for the both of us without either side getting stupid about it. That's all I'm saying. We're not here to take over. Just doing our thing."

"That itself may present a bit of a problem," Vincent said. "You see, I have business interests all over this city, including the surrounding suburbs. Most of them are not widely known. I can't just have you blindly knocking over places that may belong to me."

"One of the reasons why I'm here. Just let us know

what areas to stay clear of, or what places belong to you, and we'll skip right over them."

Vincent briefly looked at Malloy as he contemplated his options. He then stared Billings in the eyes for a minute. "I'm sure you can also see the perils of me just telling you what belongs to me. That wouldn't exactly be in my best interests."

"I'm trying to be cooperative here."

"I'll tell you what I can do. I'll assign someone to be your contact. Whatever you plan on hitting, you clear it with him first. If it's mine, or something for reasons of my own that I don't want touched, you steer clear. If it's not, you have a green light."

"I don't know if the boys are gonna like having to get permission to do what they want."

"That's my best offer," Vincent sternly said. "You're free to take it or leave it."

"I'll have to take it back to the boys and discuss it with them first if you don't mind?"

"Take all the time you need. In the meantime, if something gets hit that belongs to me before you give me your answer, you might as well not come back with one. In the same vein, if you agree to these terms, and then choose to ignore them, or don't follow them to the letter, you'll be choosing your own fate. I hope I make myself clear."

"You absolutely do. I'll take it back to the boys." Billings got up and then reached his hand across the table to shake. "It was a pleasure to meet you, sir."

Vincent once again returned the handshake. "The pleasure was all mine." Billings turned around and was about to leave before Vincent spoke up again. "Oh, before you go, you should also know that I'm not the only main player in this town."

"Oh?" Billings said. "I was under the impression you had no other rivals."

"Not in this capacity, you're right, I don't. But there are other powerful people in this city who also will not take your arrival so happily."

"If you're talking about the law, we'll deal with them when the time comes."

"I'm talking about something much bigger than the law and a hundred times more lethal."

"And what would that be?"

"There's a man who works in the city called The Silencer," Vincent said.

"Yeah, I've heard of him."

"I should warn you that he is an incredible threat."

"I think we can deal with him."

"Others have said the same."

"We're not the others," Billings said. "We have over eighty members right now. I think we can deal with one man."

Vincent grinned. "As you wish. I just felt you should be adequately warned about the dangers."

"Appreciate it. So, who is this guy? I've heard some pretty wild stories about him. What is he, some kind of jacked-up superhero?"

"Well I don't know his real name or his backstory, but I've seen his work up close. As far as I'm concerned, there is no one better."

"Sounds like you got a deep affection for this guy."

"I would love to put him on my payroll. But he marches to his own drumbeat."

"So, you two aren't on the same side."

"The Silencer is on his own side."

"So how is it that you two coexist?"

"Because he and I made an agreement long ago not to interfere in each other's business, similar to the offer I made to you. So far, we've both kept our ends of that agreement. We stay out of each other's way. I'll say it again. I'll warn you to stay out of his."

"Thanks again."

Billings then turned around again to leave. Vincent and Malloy were quiet as they watched the man exit the room.

"Make sure he exits the facilities in the proper fashion," Vincent said.

Malloy got up and left the room, making sure that Billings left without any trouble. There was always the odd chance that the Scorpions were using the meeting as a cover to get Vincent into one spot so they could take their shot at taking him out in one swift stroke. Thankfully, there would be none of that on this day. Malloy returned to the conference room a few minutes later.

"He's gone," Malloy said. "No problems."

"No problems indeed."

Malloy sat down across from his boss to further discuss the meeting. "You don't really believe all that, do you?"

"You think he came in here and lied to my face?"

"Boss, you know their reputation as well as I do. They don't peacefully coexist with nobody. If they come in here, if we let them come in here, we're eventually gonna have to deal with them. And not by talking."

"What do you propose?"

"Let them know they're not welcome here. Don't even let them get a foothold."

"They have a large group," Vincent said. "It wouldn't be an easy endeavor. And after just recently getting rid of Nowak, I'm not sure we have the stomach to take up such a task at the moment."

"Even if we're not at full strength right now, we might not have any other choice."

"There is always another choice. If we decide to throw down against this group right now, it would be like two giant behemoths in the gladiator ring, just taking turns annihilating each other. It wouldn't be pretty. And it could decimate both sides."

"What's the alternative?"

"We wait. We plan. We keep an eye on them. We don't let our guard down. We make plans to put something in place for when they get out of line, then we're able to end it quickly without it turning into a bloodbath."

"OK. We can do that. How come you didn't tell him about both Silencers?"

"I think that's something that's best left for them to discover for themselves," Vincent replied. "And if there's one thing I know about Mr. Recker and friends, I'm sure they'll be knocking on their door soon enough."

# ABOUT THE AUTHOR

Mike Ryan is a USA Today Bestselling Author. He lives in Pennsylvania with his wife, and four children. He's the author of the bestselling Silencer Series, as well as many others. Visit his website at www.mikeryanbooks.com to find out more about his books, and sign up for his newsletter. You can also interact with Mike via Facebook, and Instagram.